SCANDALOUS

KIM HARTFIELD

SCANDALOUS

Copyright © 2019 Kim Hartfield

ISBN: 9781090941848.

One – Zana

Fame was a gift and a curse. Sometimes the constant scrutiny and the lack of privacy could be annoying. Even the fans' admiration and excited squeals eventually got old. It was a relief to go somewhere that I could be anonymous for a while.

Like the ski resort where I was currently vacationing in Banff. The ski goggles hid my well-known wide blue eyes, and the helmet concealed my thick waves of platinum blonde hair – although at the moment, both were off as I sat in the ski lodge and Tia placed a beer in front of me.

"This one's for that backflip you pulled off back there." She touched my shoulder, squeezing gently. "That was epic!"

"I shouldn't drink," I said. "I'm still planning to go back out there."

"Go back out?" Kaidee asked. "I thought we were done for the day. I wanted to stay in and get loaded." Gemini and Brittney nodded.

"Drink up," Tia said. Her hand was on my knee now, and her eyes sparkled at me. I could almost hear the part she wasn't saying: that she wanted to get me back to the cabin.

I took a long sip of beer, and the other girls cheered. "Don't get me wrong," I said. "I'm still not done! I'm going to drink this and get back out. I want to give Razor Cliff another try."

"No! Baby…" Tia ran a finger up my leg, giving me puppy-dog eyes.

Half the people on the planet would've killed to be in my position. Tia's soft features deliciously contradicted her curvaceous body. She was an international sex symbol for good reason.

But I was unmoved. "I have to," I said. "It defeated me last year, and I've been dying for another chance ever since."

"You've been drinking." Gemini pointed at my half-empty pint glass. "Try Razor Cliff tomorrow."

"I plan to try it both days." I swigged down the rest of the beer. "This didn't even get me tipsy. I'll be fine."

"Zana…" Tia stroked my arm.

"You guys will be fine, too. I'm not dragging you with me." I stood up, my ski boots clunking heavily against the floor.

The ski lodge was teeming with people, and as I stepped toward the door, a woman at the next table over rushed in front of me. She was around me and my friends' age, but much less attractive.

"Oh my God, I thought it was you," she said. "Zana King, right? Oh my *God*, Tia DeSoul, you're here too! You two are the absolute cutest couple. I follow both of you on Twitter!"

"Thanks," I said, already bored.

"Guess we're chopped liver," Kaidee muttered to the other two.

She was basically right. Even though the three of them had a few thousand Instagram followers, they weren't what I would call "famous." No one got starstruck and freaked out at the sight of them.

Even Tia was less famous than me. Despite having no discernible talents, she'd parlayed a reality TV stint into name recognition that had already lasted for a few years. Dating me helped her stay in the public eye.

"So you're skiing?" the woman asked. "You ski?"

"Yeah, I was just about to get back out there." I glanced back at Tia, suppressing a smirk. "But maybe Tia has time to talk to you."

I headed for the door, bracing myself against the bitter cold. After putting on my skis, I followed the signs for Razor Cliff – the most challenging ski run at this resort. The double black diamond rating warned that this was for expert skiers only.

Last year I'd fallen halfway down the slope, my only fall for the entire weekend. I wanted to do it again, cleanly this time. I was going to do a backflip right off the hill where I'd fallen last year.

As I rode up the ski lift, my head felt a little fuzzy. Maybe that beer hadn't been the best idea. My balance always went to shit when I drank – so many times, I'd stumbled out of bars holding onto my friends because I couldn't stay upright.

I wondered if I should turn back. I could hang out with my crew… even sign an autograph or two. I was already at the top of the hill now, though, and the snow glimmered at me temptingly. What was the worst that could happen? If I fell again, I'd try again tomorrow.

Taking a breath, I bent at the knees and skied forward. The ground immediately sloped downward, and adrenaline rushed through me as my speed quickly picked up. The snow flew away underneath my skis, making me feel like I was flying.

Almost no one else was on the slope. It was like I was in a world of my own, all white and gleaming. A world with no cameras or paparazzi, no expectant faces or eager fans. I breathed in the crisp air, feeling an unlikely calm settle over me. Out here, alone, I could be *myself.*

I had to be a little tipsy, or I wouldn't be thinking such cheesy thoughts.

I swerved left and right, following the hill's shape. A small hill appeared, and I caught a moment of airtime. Shit, was that the one where I'd fallen? Or was that further up ahead? I hadn't done my flip – although no one was here to see it anyway. I could just tell everyone that I had –

Oh, shit. Where had that turn come from? I didn't remember the path curving like that. It was okay, though. I'd just change directions. I leaned my weight on my left ski, taking the sharp turn at full speed. Another turn was ahead, coming up faster than I'd expected. I gripped my poles, bracing myself to swerve. Forget doing tricks – I just wanted to get through this.

The hill came out of nowhere, jumping out at me. *Oh, right. This was where I fell last year.* Those were my last thoughts before I flew again.

My body twisted in mid-air before I hit the ground with a series of sickening cracks.

Two – Lacey

The woman in the bed looked nothing like the pictures I'd seen online. Half of her body was wrapped in pale blue casts, and her neck was encased in a thick white brace. Her face was a mass of purple and yellow bruises.

Her doctor's report said she'd been in a skiing accident. She'd broken her right arm in three places, her right leg in four, as well as fracturing her neck. If I hadn't already known, I would've thought she'd been in a car accident.

"Hi there," I said, approaching the bed. "You must be Zana. I'm Lacey. I'll be looking after you for the next little while."

She was sitting up straight, her back against the headboard with a massive TV positioned directly in front of her bed. Her eyes turned toward me, but I wasn't in her line of vision. Of course she couldn't move her head. I'd never worked for someone in this exact situation before – most of my patients were elderly, and weak rather than injured.

I moved in front of her so she could see me. Her gaze fixed on me, and her eyes narrowed as she took me in.

Wait, could she even talk right now? I mentally scanned through what the file had said. I'd pretty much memorized it, and as far as I could remember, it hadn't said anything about that.

"Lacey?" she rasped out.

"Yes." I gave her a quick smile. As much as I already disliked her, I was still going to be polite and professional. "I'm here to help you eat, bathe, dress, take your medications… basically to help keep you comfortable until you're all healed."

To put it even more basically, I was going to be like her servant, subject to her every whim. This was definitely going to be different from my usual assignments. Zana was like a princess in her castle, living in a mansion she owned herself at the age of twenty-one.

The place was ridiculous, a gabled white building that sprawled over a huge amount of land in downtown LA. I'd shaken my head as soon as I pulled my car into the circular driveway, and my disdain had only grown when Zana buzzed me inside. This house was the epitome of excess, and only someone who'd been drowning in wealth since birth would've thought it was an appropriate place for one person to live.

"Great," Zana said. Even with the hoarseness of her voice, I could clearly tell her tone was flat. "I'm definitely going to be comfortable when my body's just been practically snapped in half."

I blinked. Some of my patients with dementia didn't understand why I was there. Zana did, and she was meeting me with hostility anyway.

"Bit short-sighted to antagonize the one person who has the power to make your life miserable," I said. "Isn't it?"

Her lips tightened, and she turned her eyes away. "Who sent you?"

"Planning to fire me already?"

Her gaze snapped back to me. "Who? My mom, my dad? Both?"

"Neither, actually." I'd been pretty surprised when I realized Zana King was going to be my next patient. "The person who interviewed me was some guy named Gary."

"Ah… my mom's assistant." She looked unimpressed. "Makes sense, he brought me home from the hospital. Anyway, there's a bottle of painkillers on the nightstand. Make yourself useful and pop one in my mouth, would you?"

"Sure. Are you in pain?" I took the bottle.

"No shit, Sherlock." She opened her mouth as I placed the pill inside.

God, this assignment was going to be a long one. "How's the pain on a scale of one to ten?" I reached for the glass of water that'd been next to the pill bottle.

"I don't know. Like, a hundred?" She waved away the water with her good hand, swallowing the pill dry.

I sat heavily on the bed, leaning over her so I

could look into her eyes again. She gave a yelp, and I wondered if I'd hurt her. Too bad if I had. This entitled celebrity brat had never had a problem before in her life. She could deal with a little pain.

"Look, we need to set some ground rules," I said. "You don't have to like me. You don't even have to respect me. But my job is to take care of you, and when I'm trying to do that job, I need you to not get in the way."

Her eyes were huge, her lips slightly parted. "It was just a…"

"Joke?" I shook my head. "I didn't find it funny. You want me to write down 'one hundred' in your chart here? Then tomorrow, when I ask you the same question, how am I going to compare what you say then?"

"Okay." Her voice quivered. "Fine. Whatever."

"So, if one is no pain, and ten is the worst pain you've ever felt…"

"That'd be the moment I hit the ground." She pursed her lips. "Right now, with the painkillers kicking in… maybe a six, honestly."

"All right." I wrote it down, biting back the rest of what I wanted to say. *Was that so hard?*

I didn't know what I'd expected. Of course Zana was going to be nothing like the rest of my patients. She was twenty-one – two years younger than me – and lived a completely different lifestyle from the older people I normally cared for.

I still wasn't sure why her mother's assistant had chosen me for the gig. My agency had probably been low on more experienced workers. With the aging population, there were always more people needing care than those ready to provide it.

Well, I'd do the best job I could. I didn't have to like or respect Zana to do that. Which was good, because I didn't.

Who was she to be so entitled and rude? She'd done nothing more impressive than I had. In fact, seeing as she probably hadn't worked a day in her life, she'd done less.

Her parents were talented. Colette King, the singer – some of her heartfelt ballads were classics, and I'd always remember slow-dancing to *Journey of the Heart* in middle school. And Maurice King, the actor who'd now become a director. His action movies were always entertaining, whether he was behind or in front of the camera. I was pretty sure he'd won Oscars for both.

Together, they were one of the cutest couples in Hollywood. They'd been together for ages, since the start of both of their careers. There'd never been a hint of them getting divorced, no scandals drifting around them. They were known for being in love, with each other and with their daughter.

Zana was famous for nothing more than being

the combination of their genes, and while that might've been enough for some people, it didn't impress me.

"So, are you going to get off my bed?" she asked. "Or were you planning to sit there all day?"

I tried not to throw her a dirty look. "Here's a bell." I placed it near her good hand. "Ring it if you need me."

"Yeah…" She pushed it off the nightstand. "I won't be doing that."

THREE – ZANA

As best as I could without turning my head, I watched Lacey leave the room. How far was she going? How was I going to call her without the bell?

God, pushing it over had been a dumb thing to do. Not much of a surprise – I was no stranger to impulsiveness or reckless decisions. Like how I got here. *Ugh…*

I could've killed my mother for saddling me with a home care worker. It was just like her. Heaven forbid she come home from her latest tour or song-writing retreat or wherever the hell she was at the moment – I didn't even bother to pay attention anymore – and take care of me herself.

Wasn't that what mothers *did?* Didn't that maternal instinct just appear when you gave birth? It seemed like something any of my friends' moms would've done without even being asked, without even hesitating. Of course, my friends' moms weren't the legendary Colette King.

I sighed. I had to pull myself together and stop whining to myself. That would only make my recovery less pleasant, and it was already unpleasant enough. Half of my body was throbbing at any given moment.

At least things were better now than they'd been that first day. I'd been in such utter agony as I lay on the ground, I could barely raise my head to yell at the next skier going by. I passed out from the pain when they came to airlift me away.

At the hospital in Banff, they'd pumped me full of painkillers, but by that point I kept looking around, trying to figure out where Tia and my friends were. I'd thought they would've raced to my side as soon as they could, but apparently they hadn't.

Tia made an appearance in the evening, stopping by to hold my hand for about ten minutes. She said the others had settled in for the night and would visit the next day. Her face filled with disgust whenever she tried to look into my eyes, and soon she made her excuses as well.

I was trying not to take it personally. I probably would've reacted the same if I'd seen her looking this way. I'd seen myself in the mirror – I looked horrible. Plus we'd only been together for six months. It wasn't like we were married. I wouldn't have expected her to stay with me all night.

Even if it'd fucking sucked being alone.

I sighed again, harder this time. I wondered if people were talking about me online. I hoped the world knew the kind of misery I was going through. Hopefully people were tweeting sympathetic things at me. It wouldn't actually help, but it'd be nice to know someone out there cared about me – even just strangers.

"Hey," I called.

There was no response.

"Hey!"

I waited a long moment, then opened my mouth to shout louder. Lacey could be anywhere by now – exploring one of the four guest bedrooms, or downstairs helping herself to the contents of my fridge. Or she could've decided to go for a dip in my indoor pool. I braced myself before starting to shout. The effort was already making pain throb through the break in my neck.

Lacey's voice came from the doorway. "I have a name, you know."

I flicked my eyes in her direction. Without being able to turn my head, I couldn't see her. "So?"

"My name's not 'hey.' If you're going to shout for me, it'd be nice if you used it."

I grimaced, and not from the discomfort this time. "Are you serious? You said I don't have to respect you."

"I know you know my name. You used it earlier." From the sound of her voice, she hadn't moved an inch closer.

Fuck… "Lacey," I bit out. "Would you hand me my tablet?"

Without a word, she did. Then she placed the

bell back on the nightstand. "In case you need it."

Was that smugness on her face? God, I'd barely met her and I was already sick of her. I might just look into firing her after all. I was sure Gary could find someone else in about a minute. My mother had to be paying top dollar for this so-called service.

She was cute – that was the one good thing I could say about her. She had nothing on Tia, obviously, but she was tall and solidly built, with strong features and wide-set eyes. Her brown hair was in a high bun. Vaguely, I wondered how long it was.

Now that I had the tablet, I swiped at the screen with my good hand, unlocking it so that it prompted me for the password. I started to put it in, pecking it out letter by letter. Since I couldn't bend my neck, I could barely see what I was doing. Before I could finish, the tablet slid off the side of my lap. I tried to block it with my right-hand cast, but without the use of my fingers, there wasn't much I could do.

Twisting awkwardly, I picked the tablet up with my left hand and started the process again. This time, I didn't get through two letters of the password before it fell.

I closed my eyes. Checking social media could wait until later. I had a more pressing need.

"Lacey?" I called. "Hey, Lacey!"

She came much faster this time, planting herself in my line of vision. "Yes, Zana?"

I resisted the urge to kick that smug smile off her face with my good foot. Swallowing my pride, I muttered, "I need to pee."

"Sure." She glanced over my body, then pulled the covers off me. Surprisingly, the movement didn't hurt, even though part of the blanket had been under me. Maybe she was halfway decent at her job after all.

"I'm going to turn you toward the edge of the bed, and then you're going to pull yourself forward, okay?" she asked.

I nodded. "My crutches are around here somewhere." I'd gotten fairly good at using them during the days I'd been in the hospital.

"We're not going to bother with those. You can just lean on me."

"I'd kind of rather… If you…"

She gave me a hard stare. "It's easier this way. You don't have to be embarrassed. I've heard people pee before."

I twisted toward the side of the bed, hoping I'd somehow, magically be able to get up and walk to the bathroom, proving I didn't need her after all. Unfortunately, all that happened was that I moved about an inch and ended up breathless.

"Ready to do it my way?" Lacey asked.

"Fine," I grumbled.

Once I was up, I tugged at the bottom of my nightgown. It was a cute yellow thing, a T-shirt style that came down to my knees and flattered my figure – or usually did. In my current state, sweaty and pale with my face bruised and hair a mess, I doubted anyone would even think to look at my curves.

I hated to even have one person see me like this. At least it was only some random nobody. Lacey wasn't famous – there was nothing to be embarrassed of.

My broken foot touched the floor, and I let out a yell.

"Lean on me." Lacey's voice was calm. "Come on, I'm right here."

I tried to put my weight on her as I took the step, using her like a crutch. It was a long slog to the bathroom, even though it was only a few feet away. Lacey's arms were warm and strong. She didn't falter, even when I put all of my weight on her. It wasn't that I was purposely trying to throw her off-balance, but with her attitude, well… I wouldn't have minded if she stumbled.

Finally we reached the bathroom, and she got me positioned in front of the toilet. She actually looked flustered as she passed me on the way out. "We'll use your crutches on the way back."

So she'd been wrong? I'd been right? I did my business, then called her to help me to the sink. "Why didn't you think I should use the crutches?" I asked. "Don't you know what you're doing?"

"I normally care for elderly people rather than injured patients." She walked at my side as I teetered along with the crutches.

"How long have you been doing this?" We were almost back to my bed.

"A few years now. I'm saving up some money to – "

"Stop." I turned, putting my weight on the crutches as I swiveled my body. "I don't give a fuck. I'm trying to figure out if you're qualified to be here. I don't need your entire life story."

She wasn't in my line of vision, so I didn't know how my words affected her, but the "oh-*kay*" she let out said a lot. There was irritation there, definitely. Embarrassment. A hint of pain.

"I think you are qualified." I dropped heavily to the bed. "But I'm still making up my mind."

Her eyes met mine, and something passed between us.

Maybe, just maybe, we'd manage to get through this.

FOUR – LACEY

Day two. I walked into Zana's mansion with a fake smile on my face, already looking forward to the end of the twelve-hour shift.

I'd complained to my mom about my new patient until she told me to shut up and stop whining. At least I had a job, she said, and a decently-paying one at that. I understood where she was coming from. Now that my three older siblings had moved out, it was just me, her, and my dad paying the rent. Neither had an education, so they both worked for close to minimum wage. My income was necessary to keep us in our rental house.

"Morning, sunshine," I said to Zana. She was positioned much the same as she'd been when I left last night, sitting up with her back against the headboard.

"Hi." She glared at me from above her neck brace.

"How you feeling?" I picked up her chart and glanced over her overnight care worker's notes. We'd met briefly on my way out, and she seemed pleasant and competent. "Pain, scale of one to ten?"

She grimaced. "Four."

"Anything special happen overnight?"

"Nope." She scratched at her arm as if trying to get under the cast. "I do need you to help me use my tablet."

"I gave it to you yesterday."

"I can't use it one-handed." She gave me a sulky look, which didn't make me any more inclined to help her. Unfortunately, that was what I was getting paid to do.

"Fine," I said, grabbing the tablet from the nightstand and sitting cross-legged on the bed beside her. "What's your password?"

"ZaNa98. Capital Z, capital N."

Her own name was her password? I kept quiet, even though I wanted to say something sarcastic. "All right. What now?"

"My texts." She kept her eyes on the screen as I held it in front of her. "Open the messaging app."

"Okay, there's two from someone named Kaidee, one from Gemini…"

"Forget those. Isn't there anything from Tia?"

I double-checked. "No."

Her face tightened. "The app must not be working right."

I was pretty sure it was, but I wasn't going to say anything. It would've been unprofessional and just plain mean.

"Would you call her for me?" she asked. "My

phone's on the nightstand. Dial her and put it on speakerphone."

I nodded. "Sure."

As the phone rang, I placed it on her lap. I waited beside her in case Tia didn't pick up. After the fourth ring, she did, and yet I stayed where I was.

"Zana?" Tia asked through the phone. "I've been waiting to hear from you." There was noise in the background, which quieted after a few moments.

"You have?" Zana sounded softer now, vulnerable. "I thought you'd text me."

"Why would I text you when you wouldn't be able to use a phone?" Tia scoffed. "I just assumed you'd give me a call when you were feeling up to it."

Zana's face filled with relief. "It's good to hear your voice. I've missed you."

"Me too. You're missing out on so much stuff. The crew and I went out last night. They were all asking about you."

"And what'd you say?"

"That you're good and you're out of the hospital." Tia sounded a little odd, almost defensive.

A moment went by before Zana spoke again. "I thought you might come visit me now that I'm out."

"I will," Tia quickly said. "Soon."

"Good, because I'm fucking bored and in pain, and…" Her eyes darted toward me. "I have these fucking babysitters watching me around the clock."

"Oh, you have someone looking after you?"

"Yeah, my mom hired these women. I can't even pee alone." Her voice rose. "I can't even talk to my own goddamn girlfriend alone."

I sprang off the bed. I hadn't meant to stay in her space. I'd just been a little curious.

I cared less about celebrity gossip than just about anything else in the world, but even I'd heard of Zana's relationship with Tia DeSoul. They were one of the best-known lesbian couples out there, and I guessed I'd been a little curious to see if they were really as happy as they seemed.

The answer appeared to be no.

"Ring when you need me," I whispered.

I stepped into the hall and sank to the floor's plush carpeting. Everything in Zana's mansion looked so expensive, I didn't even want to go into any other rooms. Plus if I was further away, it'd be harder to hear her, and if there was ever an emergency, it'd take me longer to get to her.

Even though I wasn't trying to eavesdrop, I could still hear her conversation. "I'm sorry to be a bitch," Zana was saying. "My life is just a pile of shit at the moment, and I needed to vent a little. Being in constant pain is really putting me in a bad mood."

I was surprised she had that kind of self-awareness. As far as I'd been able to tell, she was a complete and unadulterated brat.

"It'll get better," Tia said soothingly. "How long are you going to be healing?"

"At least six to eight weeks."

"That's not so bad."

"Easy for you to say!" Zana's frustration was audible. "You're still out there walking around like nothing ever happened."

"Except I don't have you with me, and that sucks."

I wondered if Zana could hear the note of insincerity in Tia's voice.

"Right," Zana sighed. "Fuck, I wish you'd come here."

"Soon," Tia said.

"Like today?"

"I have a hair appointment, or I'd be there."

I shifted on the floor, uncomfortable just listening to this. What kind of excuse was that? She couldn't cancel a hair appointment to visit her invalid girlfriend?

"Okay," Zana said slowly. "Tomorrow, maybe?"

"Sure, baby. I'll be there."

Why did I already feel like she was lying?

"See you tomorrow," she went on.

"Wait, you're going?" Zana asked. "I thought we could talk for a while. I – I have nothing else to do."

"Sorry," Tia said. "I'd love to, but I have to go. I'm out shopping with Brittney, and she's waiting for me in the dressing room. We have to pick her out a hot outfit for tonight."

"Oh." Zana's voice was small. "Okay."

"I'll send you pictures of the choices, okay? It'll be like you're right here with us."

"All right," Zana said. "I'll be wait – "

"Bye, baby." The dial tone sounded.

I stood up, expecting Zana to call me in to take the phone off her lap. She didn't make a sound, so I hovered where I was. After a moment, I did hear something – a sniffle, and then another.

Fuck, I didn't want to feel sorry for her. I replayed her words in my mind. *I have these fucking babysitters watching me around the clock. I can't even talk to my own goddamn girlfriend alone.*

Venom built inside me, and I nodded to myself.

Yep, I still couldn't stand her.

FIVE – ZANA

Tia didn't come to visit me the next day, claiming an urgent situation had come up. I wasn't sure what that might've been, considering she didn't have a job.

We spoke on the phone again, but like the last time, she was busy and made an excuse to cut our call short. Not that I cared *that* much. Conversation had never been the main focus of our relationship, always coming in second to sex. Right now, our conversations were even more stilted. I could only talk so much about how my situation sucked, and I couldn't muster much of an interest in the everyday things that were going on with her.

I texted and talked to my other friends a little, but they seemed busy too. Or maybe I just bored them. They asked how I was, and then I asked what they were up to, and then the conversation with each of them tapered out.

So I sat in bed watching Netflix for hours on end, one season of *Peace and Justice* after another. By the time my body healed, I was practically going to have a law degree.

At least watching TV was something I could do by myself. For anything else, from eating to using the bathroom, Lacey or the overnight worker had to help me.

The overnight one was fine – probably because I slept through most of her shifts. Her name was Karen, and she was a fifty-something woman who seemed more interested in her own beauty rest than helping me. I could've complained about the amount that she slept, but honestly, I didn't give a shit. Whenever I needed something, I yelled at her to wake up, and she helped me in silence before going straight back to the closest guest bedroom.

Lacey was more annoying, probably because of her doe-eyed diligence.

She looked over my charts on the fourth morning. "I see Karen bathed you two nights ago. Would you want to have another shower soon?"

"Uh, let me think. Do I reek like a sewage plant?" I raised my good arm. "You tell me. I can't turn my head."

Lacey brought the crutches to the edge of the bed. "If you wanted to shower, you could've said something."

"Whatever." It wasn't like my stench mattered, considering that no one came to see me. "Just no filming."

"Of course I'm not going to film you!"

"There's no 'of course' about it. The paycheck from TMZ would set you up for life."

I'd learned early on that nothing in my life was private. Everything I said or did was up for grabs, all because of who my parents were.

They'd done their best to keep me sheltered, to the extent that they'd been around. All of my nannies and au pairs had been instructed to keep me away from TV and computer screens, but as a curious kid, I tried to find ways around it.

One of my first memories was of reporters pointing cameras in my face as I walked outside with my parents. They'd called my name and asked me questions. My mom had picked me up, pressing my face into her chest, when I tried to answer. She seemed to be mad at me, but I hadn't known any better.

I quickly learned I wasn't like the kids on TV, or the ones in the books I read. Normal kids, who went to real schools and had friends their own age. I had a teacher who came to my house every day, making me sit in a single desk in one of our living rooms and getting mad whenever I lost focus for even a minute.

I'd socialized with other celebrity kids on the rare occasion that my parents thought to set up a play date. That was the thing – they didn't think of me that often. They bought whatever I needed, anything money could buy. And there were a lot of things that it couldn't.

It was a miracle I'd turned out as well-adjusted as I had.

I must've been about eight when I'd seen my face in a newspaper for the first time. One of the nannies must've left it lying around, or maybe I'd dug it out of the recycling bin. I knew I wasn't supposed to look at it, but when did that ever stop a kid?

My picture was on the front page of the entertainment section. *Zana King Makes A Splash With Auburn Hair,* the headline said. I'd had my hair dyed a few days earlier – my mom had brought her stylist to the house. But it was *my* hair. Why would anyone else care?

A sick feeling grew in my stomach as I read the article. It called me a trendsetter, a fashionista. It talked about how little girls all over the country might dye their hair auburn to look like me, the way they'd all hopped on the crimped-hair trend I'd supposedly started. The article wasn't long, and I didn't need to sound any words out, and yet it still left me utterly confused.

I hobbled into the bathroom using the crutches and sat heavily on the closed toilet while Lacey pulled out the cast covers. The best money could buy, no plastic-bagging for me. It was too bad money couldn't buy this pain away or heal these bones any faster.

"I'm not here to exploit you," she said, fixing a cover around my broken leg. "You should know I signed an NDA, since you're so worried."

"Right," I mumbled, holding my arm out for her to put the cover over it. "And I'm sure there's no chance you'll tell the media what you hear me talk about on the phone."

She looked me in the eye. "I'm here to do my job, and that's all."

I wished I could trust her, but I'd been burnt too many times. Like when I was eleven and my parents found out my au pair was writing a tell-all book about my family. Or when I thought I made a friend in high school, and then she snapped an upskirt picture when I was getting into her boyfriend's car.

I hadn't done anything for people to be interested in me, and yet they were – often fanatically. I'd done nothing more than be born and exist, and people chased after every tidbit of information about me, devoured them like crumbs of food and they were starving.

"All right," Lacey said. "Lift your butt."

Leaning on my good foot, I allowed her to pull the nightgown from under my ass.

"Arms up."

Making a face, I lifted them. She raised the fabric over my head, folded it, and set it on the sink.

"Get a good look," I said as she started to cover my neck brace. "People would pay a lot of money to get the view you have right now."

She kept her eyes on my face. "Good thing I'm not 'people.'"

I started to scoff as she guided me to sit in the chair in the shower, but the sound was silenced by my breath catching in my throat. It felt good to have a pretty girl's hands on me, even if this was the least sexual situation I could imagine. I guessed it'd been too long since I'd seen Tia.

"God, how does this thing even work?" she asked.

Like most things in my place, my shower was on the fancier side. Three showerheads hung from above us, ready to blast us with water from all directions. The one-way glass window looked over the city from floor to ceiling, giving us one of the best views in the house. It was bright and sunny outside, nothing like it'd been in Banff.

"The controls are there," I said, pointing.

After pushing up her sleeves, she turned on the water. I put my hand under the spout to check the temperature. When it was good and hot, I pulled the handle to make the water come out of the showerhead.

Lacey yelped and jumped back. "You really like it hot!"

I chuckled to myself. "You can say that again."

She was doing her best to stay out of the spray, but she was still getting soaked. With the neck brace preventing my head from turning, I couldn't get a good eyeful of the way her clothes stuck and clung to her curves, but when she darted in front of me, I got a hint of what was going on.

Damn, she had a nice body – sturdy yet still feminine. Her hair was getting wet, too, and a strange impulse made me want to yank it out of its bun.

"I'm going to soap you up," she said. "Do you like to use a washcloth, or…" She hesitated, sounding thrown off for once. Rubbing me down seemed to be too much for her usual professionalism.

"I can use my good hand," I said. "You've done enough."

She still seemed unsure. "What about cleaning your good side? I better stay and help."

"You really want to touch me all over, huh?" I grabbed for the soap, which was well out of my reach. "Just remember I have a girlfriend."

She gave me the bar, and between the two of us, we worked in silence to get me clean. She only helped with the parts I couldn't reach myself, and yet I had to admit I liked the way her hands felt on my body.

After, she looked at the controls again. It took her a minute to figure out how to turn the shower off. I watched her fiddle around with them. If she wasn't going to ask me for help, I wasn't about to offer it.

Still soaked, she helped me into a fluffy bathrobe. "Would you mind if I borrowed something to wear?" she asked. "Just until the end of my shift. I figure I'll throw my clothes in your dryer."

"Fine," I said, clomping to my bed. "Find

something in my closet. Nothing with a designer label. And no 'oops, I forgot to return it.' I'm going to write down what you borrow and what you return."

She didn't answer, just strode away.

Was I too harsh on her? I did my best to pull the blankets over myself, feeling guilty at the tone I'd used.

Lacey had never done anything to make me distrust her.

But why would she be different from everyone else I'd ever met?

Six – Lacey

At half past nine, I turned into my parents' driveway. On leaden feet, I walked into the house and sat heavily at the kitchen table. My mouth opened in an unstoppable yawn.

These twelve-hour days were killing me. Nine am to nine pm, with a half-hour commute either way – I hardly had time left to live. The money was good, and the gig wasn't forever, but how could I handle six-plus weeks like this? I wasn't even through the first week, and I was sorely tempted to kick Zana in her already-broken leg.

Her attitude was half of the problem, of course. I was just about sick of her constant rudeness. Even if I felt sorry for her, that wasn't enough to make up for the way she treated me. And I couldn't feel all that sorry for her when she'd actually caused her injuries herself.

Sighing, I heaved myself up. The sink was full of dishes, and the floor needed a good sweep. My mom must not have had time to clean up. She worked as many hours as I did right now, and not just temporarily. Between his two jobs, my dad also came close. It wouldn't have been fair for me to leave this mess for one of them.

I'd barely touched the broom when Mom padded into the kitchen. Already in her bathrobe, her hair in curlers, she moved to take the broom away from me. "No, no, no," she said. "You've worked hard enough."

"So have you," I said, pulling the broom out of her reach. "I'm not having this fight with you. Go sit down and relax."

"That's what I've been doing." She coughed out a laugh – she'd been a smoker for too long. "That's why all this mess is still here. I should've finished before you came."

I was going to have to compromise, even though I didn't want to. She looked older and frailer with every passing day, but she wasn't going to take no for an answer.

"Why don't you wash the dishes while I sweep?" I asked.

She started filling the sink. "You know you don't have to help. You've had a long day."

"Doing easy work." I pushed the broom, disgusted by the amount of grime that had already accumulated. "I spend most of the day sitting on my butt, waiting for that girl to need me. You actually work your butt off." She worked at a high school cafeteria, cooking and serving food to ungrateful teens.

"Even easy work can be tiring."

I shrugged, not that she was looking at me. "I used to do the same kind of thing for free. At least I'm making money now."

"May your grandmother rest in peace."

I kept sweeping despite the wave of sadness that came over me. I missed Grandma every day, but I'd started missing her long before she passed away. Her last few years had been plagued by dementia, along with all the physical problems that came along with aging.

She'd forgotten who I was, often calling me by my mother's name. She was always confused about where she was, sometimes even wandering into the street. She'd been a shell of the vibrant woman I'd once known, and a little more of her had withered away every day.

When pneumonia finally took her last winter, it'd almost been a relief. At least she wasn't suffering anymore – and we could remember her the way she once was, rather than watching her real self slip away little by little.

I finished sweeping the kitchen and set the broom against the wall. I'd get to the other rooms in a second. The one good thing about the three of us being squeezed into this small space was that it meant less area to clean.

Mom glanced at me. "So the work is okay?" she asked mildly, still washing dishes. "That girl is still rude?"

"She's all right," I said carefully, not wanting to let her know how bad it was. "She's just… she's never worked a day in her life, and you can tell."

"Hmm." Mom set the last dish in the drying rack and turned to face me. "They say celebrities are just like us."

"I guess so." Richer than us, for sure. Ruder, more spoiled, less respectful… "Just like us."

*

I kept waking up that night, and each time I yelled at myself. The less I slept, the harder the next day was going to be. If I found Zana frustrating on a full eight hours' sleep, she was going to be impossible if I was exhausted.

Grabbing my phone, I went on the Internet. Thoughts of Zana were keeping me from sleeping, and Googling her wouldn't help, but somehow I couldn't stop myself from doing it.

A bunch of articles from celebrity gossip sites popped up, all featuring similar headlines.

Zana King Recovering Post-Skiing Accident.

Zana King's Broken Bones: A Complete List.

Zana King Reappears On Twitter After Ski Crash.

I clicked the last one, which was dated from yesterday. My heart raced as I saw how many tweets she'd apparently sent out. Would she have said something about me? Complained about how I was making her life miserable?

I scanned through the tweets, not seeing any mention of my name. Somewhat soothed, I went back to the top and read through them.

Stuck in bed watching Peace & Justice. Ugh!

Never been so bored in my life! Or in so much PAIN!

Only good thing about today is the cupcakes & flowers Tia sent me. Best girlfriend ever!

The tweets were as vapid and shallow as I would've expected. Only two things stood out.

First, that she hadn't seen any reason to mention me. She had no comments about her home care worker. I didn't stand out enough to get a Twitter mention, even though I spent twelve hours a day at her side. I swallowed down my bitterness, wondering why I would've expected anything else. And why I even cared.

The second thing was that she'd felt the need to lie about what Tia had done. She hadn't gotten cupcakes or flowers from anyone. Why make up such a thing?

I'd already seen their relationship wasn't what it seemed to be. I shouldn't have been surprised by one more lie.

But as I pressed my face into the pillow, begging sleep to come, I wondered what exactly was in it for Zana.

Seven – Zana

Day six. T minus thirty-six days until the absolute earliest I could get these casts off. It might even be longer than that, if my bones didn't heal as well as I hoped they would. My pain had abated so that it was mostly a dull throb I didn't notice unless I happened to pay attention.

I'd been in a bad mood for the past six straight days. I was used to playing sports and jogging for miles. Now I couldn't even step out of bed on my own. My casts chafed and my head ached, and all the strength I'd worked so hard to build was disintegrating.

But there was nothing I could do – I just had to wait this out. All the money in the world couldn't buy a way to make this time pass any faster.

"Lacey!" I hollered, shifting around in my bed.

She walked in front of me so I could see her. She was always so quick to respond, much quicker than Karen.

"How do you always get here so fast?" I asked suspiciously. "Do you just sit in the hall, or something?"

"Well, yes." She spoke as if that was a perfectly normal thing to do. "What if you had an emergency?"

"Seriously? I have broken bones. I'm not a damn invalid."

She cracked a smile. "Pretty sure that's the definition of an invalid, Zana."

I wasn't sure if I'd seen her smile before. I must've, but not a real smile like this one. It looked good on her – even if it meant she was laughing at me. I kind of wanted to see her look this happy more often.

"Bring a chair in the hall. No point in both of us being uncomfortable." I waved my good hand at her as she started to move away. "I don't mean right now! I want some chips."

"You want?"

Fuck… Karen never made me jump through stupid hoops like this. "You told me I didn't have to respect you," I said.

She smirked. "We're going to be spending a lot of time together. I changed my mind."

"Fine. *Please* bring me some chips," I said, like a goddamn five-year-old.

Lacey nodded. "You got it."

She headed to the kitchen while I seethed. I was still her boss – well, my mother was, but I could have her fired anytime I wanted. I didn't have to be polite to her if I didn't feel like it. She had no right to make me say "please" to her. None!

And yet, as annoyed as I was, I wasn't quite

ready to get rid of her.

"What do you do out there?" I asked when she deposited a bag of chips in my lap.

She blinked. "In the world?"

"In the hall."

"Oh." She looked self-conscious. "I sit and read on my phone."

"That sounds boring as fuck." When she didn't answer, I pressed on. "The sound of the TV doesn't bother you?"

"A little."

"Bring the chair in here." The words came out of me before I could bite them back. "You can watch the show with me."

"Peace and Justice? I'll take a pass."

She was giving me an out, which I should've taken. I didn't really want her to sit and watch TV with me... did I? "I can pick something else. I was just about sick of that one." I was being way too nice right now. "I'll pick the next show, though. Not you."

Lacey kept her eyes on mine for a long moment, making me feel like she was looking right into my soul. Could she see how lonely I was from having no other company? Could she guess that I was disappointed that no one had come to visit?

It wouldn't take a genius to figure that out. I was going on a week without talking to anyone in person other than her or Karen, who was even less interesting. My loneliness and boredom were reaching desperate proportions.

Lacey reached up as if to play with a strand of hair, as if she'd forgotten it was all tied up in that tight bun she wore. "What kind of shows do you like?"

"Something good," I said curtly. "I'm going to browse around Netflix."

"I heard *Doctor Files* is good," she said. "Lots of seasons. I always figured I'd check it out when I had time to really sink my teeth into it."

"I told you, I'm picking the show."

Shrugging, she left the room. Was she ditching me? Would she really rather sit in the hallway playing on her phone than watch TV with me? Trying not to feel too rejected, I fumbled with the TV remote with my left hand. I scrolled through Netflix's suggestions. Nothing particularly stood out to me.

A loud thump came from the other room, and then another. I sat up as best as I could. Even if I couldn't see what Lacey was doing, I could guess she was bringing a chair here, like I'd told her to. She hadn't abandoned me after all.

The thumping got closer. "I'm back," Lacey said, breathless. "Did you decide what show you want?"

A thumbnail at the bottom of the screen caught my eye. "It's suggesting *Doctor Files*," I said. "I guess we might as well check it out."

*

Three episodes later, my bag of chips was empty and I was thoroughly addicted to the show. It'd started off slow, but quickly ratcheted up the drama until I couldn't even believe what I was seeing.

"Are you hooked?" I asked. "I'm hooked."

"I'm a little hooked," Lacey admitted. "I just love Patti. What a strong, powerful woman."

"I like Kiara more."

"For real? She's too competitive."

I scoffed. "What's wrong with being competitive? Competitions are fun."

"They can be, but not when you're supposed to be working together. People could die if Kiara keeps worrying about her own reputation more than giving the best care to her patients."

This conversation was getting serious now. It was probably the longest conversation we'd had so far – definitely the longest that wasn't about my shower controls or my bathroom habits. Which was because Lacey was my home care worker, and she was getting paid to be here.

"Help me get up," I said curtly. "I need to pee."

"Sure." Lacey sounded a bit taken aback, as if

she'd caught my sudden shift in mood.

"Then I want dinner," I said. "You can bring me the chef's menu and I'll decide what you should ask for." The chef came by three times a day to cook whatever I wanted from a preapproved, health-friendly menu.

"All right." She pulled me to the edge of the bed, her face serious as she placed the crutches on either side of me.

It was already strange and awkward to have a pretty girl taking care of me. I wasn't going to confuse things by pretending we were actually friends.

EIGHT – LACEY

Absolutely ADDICTED to Doctor Files! Zana's latest tweet read. *Why did nobody tell me about this sooner?!*

I set my phone on the nightstand and set my elbows on the chair arms, leaning forward to stare at the screen. She'd just sent that tweet while I was sitting right here, and again, she hadn't felt the need to mention she had any company.

Why would she have? It wasn't like I mattered. I was just her employee, replaceable with anyone else – even if over the past few days, we'd been talking more and more about the episodes we were watching.

We analyzed the characters, breaking down their motivations, and predicted what would come next. Sometimes we even paused the show so we could talk about it more. It felt funny to have conversations with someone who couldn't even turn her head to look at me. But the discussions were becoming more enjoyable every day.

"This man is crazy!" Zana said. "He's really going to stand Addison up? How could he?" She was beautiful, now that her bruises had faded to nothing.

"I guess he's not into her," I said mildly.

She hit pause on the remote. "That's just fucking rude. He could at least give her a call. At least send a text. There's no excuse for not doing that."

"True, but she'll get over it."

"Are you even serious? You think this is okay?"

She was getting heated, and I kind of liked pushing her buttons. Through watching the show, I'd found out she was more empathetic than she let on. She always worried about people's emotions – at least fictional people's, because she certainly didn't seem to care about mine.

We'd never talked about anything personal, and I still remembered the comment she'd made about not needing to hear my life story. That'd been the first day, when she'd been in a lot of pain, so maybe things had changed – but she still hadn't asked me anything about my life. She hadn't shown any curiosity about me whatsoever.

"Standing someone up isn't okay," I said, "but it's not the end of the world."

"Fuck that, man. Some basic respect… a little human decency… it goes a long way. That's all I'm saying."

She unpaused the show just as her phone went off with a loud sound. "What the hell is that?" I yelped.

She seemed unfazed. "Just the door buzzer."

"Someone's coming over?" I tried to keep the shock out of my voice.

If she could've looked at me, she would've glared. As it stood, her tone of voice delivered the same message. "Yes. Got a problem with that?"

"Of course not. Just…" I had my agency uniform shirt tucked in and my hair pulled up regulation-style, but she didn't look quite as respectable. She was in an orange nightgown, her front covered in chip dust. We hadn't showered her yet today, preferring to get straight into *Doc* instead, and her hair was greasy. Given how shallow her girlfriend seemed to be, I worried what'd happen if she found her like this. "Is it Tia?"

"No, my dad." She seemed to guess why I was worrying. "He's seen me look a lot worse than this. He's not going to think you're neglecting me."

I huffed out a laugh. "From now on, we'll shower you first thing in the morning."

A knock came at the door, and she waved her good hand at me. "Go open it."

"Magic word?" I said automatically.

I could almost hear the roll of her eyes. "*Please.*"

My confident attitude deserted me in the minute it took me to walk to the door. I'd gotten used to spending time with Zana, to the extent that I could almost forget who she was. Now I was about to come face-to-face with a famous actor-director, the legendary Maurice King.

I reached for the doorknob, hesitating for a moment as I plastered a smile onto my face. Celebrities were people too, like my mom had said. I mentally repeated my spiel, then threw the door open. "Hi, I'm Lacey, I'm Zana's home care worker." It all came out in one breath, making me sound as nervous as I was.

The man in the hall gave me a warm smile. "It's nice to meet you. I'm Maurice."

As if I didn't know his name! I'd seen him in more movies than I could count. He looked smaller in real life, only a few inches taller than me. His wide blue eyes looked oddly familiar for a second, and then it hit me – they were the same as Zana's.

They looked so alike, and yet he was completely different from her. How had a nice man like him given half his DNA to a rude creature like Zana? I would think her attitude came from her mom's side, but from everything I'd seen and read, Colette King was an angel sent down to Earth.

Not to mention how they were both hard-working, talented people, and Zana was... Zana.

I forced myself to take a breath. "Come on in," I said, moving out of the way for him. "Zana's looking forward to seeing you."

I didn't completely know whether that was true – she'd seemed a bit neutral about the fact that he was here – but why wouldn't she look forward to seeing him? If anything, it was odd that he'd waited until her ninth day of bed rest to come. But he was a busy man with other important things to do, things he might not be able to put on hold just because his daughter had a ski accident.

I brought him into Zana's room, and he immediately bent over the bed to give her a hug. "Hi, Maurice," she said. She didn't hug back with her good arm, I noticed.

"You look so much better than you did in the hospital," he said. "The bruises on your face are healing up."

"Right."

"Are you feeling better?"

"Much."

God, she was so short with her dad. He was finally here, and she was going to give him these one-word answers?

I cleared my throat. "Can I get you something, Mr. King? Coffee? Tea?" Maybe if I was overly polite, it'd make up for Zana's rudeness.

His eyes flickered over to me. "Some tea sounds amazing, Lacey. Something herbal, no sugar."

I practically skipped off to the kitchen. Maurice King knew my name!

When I came back, clutching the hot cup gingerly, he was already standing up. "I'm sorry, Lacey," he said. "I won't have time for that tea after all."

"Leaving so soon? You only just got here." I glanced over at Zana. Her eyes looked straight ahead, as usual, so that told me nothing about her state of mind. Her features, though, seemed unusually sullen.

"Unfortunately, yes," Maurice said. "I have to get to a meeting about my next film. The producers and I are going to be speaking with the screenwriter."

"That sounds so exciting," I breathed.

He headed to the door. "That tea does smell delicious. Maybe you'll enjoy it for me."

"It would be an honor."

Slipping his shoes on, he gave me another warm smile. "It was nice to meet you, Lacey. I'm sure I'll see you again soon."

With that, he was gone. I stood starstruck, holding my hands to my fast-beating heart.

Something felt off, and it took me a moment to figure out what it was.

In his rush to leave, he hadn't said goodbye to his daughter.

NINE – ZANA

I turned the show back on after my father left, then paused it after less than a minute.

"Hey!" Lacey said.

"I'll put it back on in a minute." I reached for my phone on the nightstand. "I'm going to make a call first, if you wouldn't mind giving me a little privacy."

From the sounds of movement, I could tell she'd jumped up and hurried out of the room. Once I was sure she was gone, I dialed Tia. Putting her on speaker, I brought my good knee to my chest and hugged it in.

"Zana?" she answered. "He-ey!"

She sounded like she was greeting an old acquaintance she didn't particularly want to talk to, not her girlfriend whose voice she hadn't heard in days.

"Hey," I said. "What's up?"

"Oh, not too much! I'm just walking Brittney's dog with her. Did you hear she's going to be in the Victoria's Secret fashion show this year?"

"No…"

"It's so great. She's been wanting to do it since forever. Gemini's hoping to get in, too, but I doubt it. Maybe if she loses those last ten pounds." I could hear Brittney in the background laughing with her.

"Want to ask how I'm doing?" I asked, sounding sharper than I'd intended.

"Of course, how are you doing?"

"Not so great."

Finally some sympathy crept into her voice. "Lots of pain?"

"No, it's not too bad. My dad just visited, and he barely stayed for five minutes. Pretty much just made sure I was alive, then jetted off for some kind of work meeting."

"Mmm."

Was she even listening? I kept talking, needing to say these words out loud, even if only to myself. "I'm so tired of him charming everyone... of the whole world thinking he's this wonderful person. He even had my home care worker wrapped around his little finger."

It'd actually hurt to see the way Lacey lapped up every bit of attention he gave her. I would've thought she was too smart to fall for his bullshit.

"They don't know him like I do," I said. "If anyone knew the kind of father he's been..."

"Your dad is so nice," Tia said. "Oh shit, look at him go!" She and Brittney exploded in laughter.

It took me a minute to work out they were talking about the dog, not my dad. She hadn't been listening at all.

"Okay, Tia," I said. "I gotta run."

"What? Oh…" She must've repositioned the phone because her voice came in clearer. "All right, baby. Talk to you later! Feel better!"

I started to hit the "call end" button, but the dial tone was already going off. Tia's goodbye echoed in my mind. She'd sounded so casual, so relaxed about everything. Shouldn't she care more about how half my body was broken and I could barely get out of bed? Shouldn't she have fucking visited me by now?

Lacey's tentative footsteps came back into the room. "It was so exciting to meet your dad." Twin thumps meant she was putting the crutches beside my bed. "We should get you into the shower."

"Did I ask for a fucking shower?" I burst out. "Or for your thoughts about my dad, for that matter?"

Although she was out of my line of vision, I could hear her wilting. "Sorry, I just – "

"What next?" I demanded. "You want to give your opinion of my relationship, too?"

"Zana, I'm sorry." She came in front of me so I could see her apologetic face. "Do you want some space?"

"You're damn right, I do."

She left me alone with my anger. And even as I stewed in it, I knew I shouldn't have taken it out on her.

*

The next day, Lacey was sitting in the hall again.
I couldn't blame her after the way I'd blown up
at her. At least she had a chair out there now,
rather than sitting on the floor. She didn't make
a peep except when I called her.

I shouldn't have cared about whether I'd hurt
her. She was *nobody*. Less than nobody. She was
there because Mom was paying her, and she'd
be gone the instant the money stopped. I still
didn't fully trust that she wouldn't find some
dirt to sell about me. People who weren't
famous were obsessed with money, and they'd
do anything for it.

But the fact was, I was bored. She'd been my
only company for ten days, aside from the brief
visit from my dad. And she'd actually been the
best company I'd had for… quite a while. I'd
enjoyed talking to her more than I cared to
admit.

I wouldn't have thought a regular person could
interest me so much. Her thoughts weren't
carefully packaged into two hundred and
eighty-character tweets, and no one I knew had
ever heard of her. But I found her perspective
refreshing. She saw things in a different way
from other people.

I guessed that was why I'd been so upset that she'd been like everyone else, falling all over herself to worship my dad.

"Lacey!" I barked out. "Get in here."

"What would you like?" she asked from the door.

She wasn't even going to object to the way I'd just talked to her? I'd kind of gotten used to her demanding "pleases" and "thank-yous." It was like banter between us now. A playful game that kept me on my toes.

"Did you know I have a follow-up appointment tomorrow?" I asked. "You're going to have to take me to the hospital."

"Oh, yes. They called and let me know."

"You sure you'll be able to get me there?" I asked. "I don't know how it's going to work."

"You have your crutches," she said. "The hard part will be getting you down the stairs. You have a driver, so once you're out the door, it's just a car ride away. You'll be fine."

"Hmm."

I didn't say anything more, and I could feel her presence at the door, waiting expectantly for my next demand.

"Anything else I can do for you?" she finally asked.

I let out a breath. "Not really."

"But kind of?"

"Well…" Still staring straight ahead, I gestured with my good hand at the TV. "These *Doc* episodes are getting pretty spicy."

"Are you inviting me to join you?"

"Sounds like it, doesn't it?"

Another pregnant pause, and then she said, "Zana, you are infuriating." I heard her drag the chair back inside the room. "If I had anything better to do, I'd be doing it. I wouldn't be sitting next to you as if I don't mind the way you talk to me, because I do mind."

"Fine by me."

As long as she was sitting in that chair, right beside my bed, where she was supposed to be.

TEN – LACEY

Getting Zana to the hospital was the easy part. She was nimble with her crutches, and once we got to the hospital, she was speeding around like it was nothing. I actually had to hurry to keep up with her.

The novelty of being out of her mansion didn't keep her from being as difficult as usual once we met the doctor. A sixty-ish man in a white lab coat, he seemed unamused by her lack of focus.

"At this point, it appears that the blood clot and callus have formed around the fracture sites," he said, then gave Zana a hard look. "That means they're healing well, but fidgeting won't help."

"Right." She stilled her leg. "So, it's still going to be six to eight weeks before I'm out of these things?"

"That depends on a few factors. Are you getting enough calcium?"

"I don't know."

"She is," I interjected. "I check her nutritional requirements daily."

The doctor looked at me with relief. "Great. And there are no chronic medical conditions, right?"

"Nope."

He spoke directly to me for the rest of the

appointment while Zana shifted around on the exam table, apparently lost in daydreams. My year and a half of nursing school had familiarized me with medical terminology, so I understood what he was saying better than she would've, anyway.

I was happy to get her out of there when we were done. She seemed volatile outside her mansion, like a chemical compound that was reacting badly to something in its new environment.

We got back into the car her mother's assistant had hired, and I told the driver to take us back to her place. Zana, though, had other ideas.

"We're going to make a stop on the way," she said, tapping the driver's shoulder until he met her eyes in the rearview mirror. "1212 Harlandale Street. Go there first and leave the meter running. We'll head to my place after."

"What are you doing?" I whispered furiously. "We can't go off gallivanting to other places. You're supposed to be on bed rest."

"Well, I've already been out of bed all morning, and I'm fine. I want to go to that address."

The driver pulled over to the side of the road. "You two need to make up your minds. Where am I taking you?"

"The address I told you," I said.

"No, the one I just gave you." Zana's voice was steely. "I'm a grown woman, Lacey. You're my care worker, not my babysitter. If I want to visit someone, we're going."

"But…"

"Do you want me to fire you over this? Because I will."

I almost laughed – almost. She hadn't threatened me with firing in a while, and I was pretty sure she wouldn't do it. We'd gotten used to each other by this point, and I knew she liked me better than her overnight worker.

Still, she had a point. It was her life, and her broken bones. If she wanted to aggravate her injuries by running around town, that was her prerogative.

"Fine," I said, then addressed the driver. "Take us where she wants to go."

When we reached our destination a few minutes later, I got out of the car to help her onto her crutches, then got back into my seat. "How long do you think this is going to take?"

"You're coming with me," Zana said, as if it was obvious.

"What? Why?" I gestured at her. Considering how she'd zoomed around the hospital, I was pretty sure she could get around fine without me.

"To… to…" She shook her head. "Just in case I need you." She plodded toward the front door.

The building seemed to be a set of condo units.

We were in the wealthy part of town, and I knew the condos in this building cost more than my family home. Like, several times more. What were we doing here? Who was she visiting?

My sense of unease built as we walked inside. I looked at the buzzer, but Zana just waved through the glass at the concierge. "They know me here."

This couldn't be her parents' place – I'd seen pictures of their opulent, expansive mansion online. There was only one person who might live here... and I wasn't completely sure if she'd want to see Zana.

We took the elevator to the penthouse floor. Questions were at the tip of my tongue – *Are you sure you know what you're doing*, and *Do you really think this is a good idea?* I kept my thoughts to myself. Like Zana had said, she was a grown woman, and she could make her own mistakes.

I just didn't particularly want to have to witness them.

Once the elevator stopped, she tapped a code into the panel. The doors slid open, and we stepped into a living room as opulent as any I could've imagined. The ceilings were about ten feet high, and thick faux fur carpeted the floors, pure white and spotless.

"She's not home yet," Zana said, dragging herself over to the couch. "We might have to wait for a while."

She talked like I was supposed to know who "she" was. "Tia?"

She nodded. "We'll just hang out here. I want to surprise her. Do you want a drink? She has a fountain."

"What, a water fountain?"

"A vodka fountain." Seeing my scandalized expression, she waved me over to the couch. "C'mon, sit."

I did, even if I resented being ordered around like a lapdog. "You know the driver is down there waiting for us, right? Do you have any respect for other people's time?"

"He's getting paid." She sounded indifferent.

I stretched my legs out. My shoes were still on, and I was sure I'd get dirt on this gorgeous carpet. Well, it didn't matter – Tia probably had someone in to clean the place daily. Wait, was I starting to think like Zana? I shook my head, disgusted at myself.

"So, I'm going to live?" she asked. "You spent a lot of time talking to that doctor."

"And you should've been listening," I said. "It's your body, not mine."

"You seemed to know what you were doing."

"Yeah, but…" I bit my tongue. There was no point in trying to teach her responsibility. If she hadn't picked it up in the past twenty-one years, it probably wasn't going to happen. "You'll be fine. You're healing normally. Just have to stay off your feet and give your body time to heal."

"How did you know all that stuff? All those words you were using with him?"

Suddenly I felt self-conscious. "I was going to be a nurse," I said slowly. "Still want to, actually."

"You'd be a good one." It had to be the first compliment she'd given me, and I was so stunned, I almost didn't hear her continue. "What got in your way?"

"Money, of course."

"So maybe after this job, you'll go back to school?"

"Exactly."

My cheeks were hot. I really wasn't used to her asking questions about me. I felt the need to be guarded – I knew she wouldn't understand anything about the struggles I'd been through, and I didn't feel like hearing her thoughts about them. Still, the fact that she was curious made me want to open up to her.

She put her elbows on her knees and leaned forward as if she was about to lean her chin in her hands. She stopped mid-lean, probably remembering her neck brace. "You should be a TV critic or something," she said. "You'd be good at that, too."

"Nursing would help more people."

"Fuck helping people." She laughed to herself.

"Have fun and make money. That's what life's all about."

The elevator beeped, and she jerked as if an electric shock had gone through her. "She's coming."

The doors opened, and a woman I recognized from online walked out. Tia looked just as gorgeous as she did in pictures, and she was as heavily made-up as she was in all of them, too. In her fur-trimmed jacket, her eyes hidden by pink aviator sunglasses, she looked like she could've just finished a photo shoot.

"Zana?" she said, not hiding her surprise. "You're here? Who is this?"

"That's just my home care worker," Zana said. "We're going to go talk in her room, Lacey."

I nodded dumbly.

Just. The word echoed in my head as they walked away.

Eleven – Zana

I teetered over to Tia's bed and slid myself onto it. She stood there watching me, not helping like Lacey would've. She didn't even take my crutches after, so I was stuck holding them on either side of me, balancing them as they tried to tip over. "Would you mind?" I pushed them toward her.

"Oh. Sure." She took them and leaned them against the wall.

I angled my body toward her so I could see her face. It was odd that she hadn't hugged or kissed me. It felt like it'd been forever since I'd seen her. It felt like I'd just invaded the home of a stranger.

"What are you doing here, Zana?" she asked.

My gut clenched as if I'd been punched. "I missed you," I said slowly. "I was out and about, I had a doctor's appointment, so I thought I'd stop by after."

"Right."

This wasn't going the way I'd expected it to at all. Why wasn't she ripping her clothes off? I'd thought this through – I wouldn't be able to use my mouth, but my left hand still worked, and she could do whatever she wanted to me.

Apparently she didn't want to do anything. She crossed her arms, looking at me with an impassive expression. She'd never looked at me like that before. From the day we'd met, introduced by mutual friends in the VIP area of an expensive nightclub, we'd only ever known passion.

"You don't mind, do you?" I asked, my voice getting smaller with each word. "I thought you'd be happy to see me."

"Zana…" She rubbed a hand over her forehead. "I don't know how to say this."

My heart dropped. Nothing good ever came after those words. "Did you meet someone else?"

"No, no. Nothing like that." A ray of hope lit up within me, and she extinguished it just as quickly. "I'm not having fun anymore, baby. This isn't fun."

"What isn't fun?"

"Being your girlfriend," she said. "Seeing you in the hospital was such a downer, and then all your calls and texts… I'm not the one with a broken neck. Why should I be the one to suffer?"

I forced myself to breathe. Tia and I had never had the deepest relationship, but I'd thought we were reasonably solid. Six months together – that was half a year! Even if it didn't sound like much, it was the longest relationship I'd been in. She was really going to dump me for not being *fun?*

"You think you're the one who's suffering?" I asked darkly. "Really? Which of us went through the kind of indescribable pain that someone who hasn't broken a bone couldn't even imagine? Which of us is walking around like nothing happened, and which is still lying in bed all day, every day, barely able to move?"

"See? That's what I mean." She shook her head. "You're a downer."

I couldn't believe what I was hearing. Tia had no empathy – none whatsoever. "You know this is temporary, right?" I asked, sounding more pathetic than I intended. "I'll be back to normal in a few weeks, and everything would go back to normal."

She shrugged. "Then let's talk in a few weeks."

"Okay…"

I thought about it, and then I got angry. I was supposed to go through the hardest thing I'd ever been through by myself, and then pretend it'd never happened? If she couldn't be there for me at my lowest point, how could I forget that when I was at my highest?

I didn't know a whole lot about love, but I knew that wasn't how it was supposed to work. If Tia cared about me, she'd be there for me right now. And I wouldn't have to nag her or harass her. She'd call and visit me willingly, because she wanted to have my company and wanted to know I was all right.

I blinked away a tear. I'd thought I meant more to her than this. Apparently I'd been wrong.

"Never mind," I said. "It's not okay. I'm just going to go now, if you could hand me those crutches."

She pushed them both at me, rather than setting me up with one on each side like Lacey would've done.

I hopped up awkwardly and maneuvered myself to the door. "Bye, Tia. Have a nice life."

*

I didn't say a word to Lacey until we were back at my place. Then I got into bed and pulled the blankets over myself. "Ice cream," I muttered. "And red wine. A lot of it. Please."

"Sure thing on the ice cream," she said. "You're not supposed to drink while your bones are healing, though."

"Fuck 'supposed to.' I want to get fucked up."

"I can't do that. The agency would have my head."

"Fine," I growled. "Then bring me double the ice cream. Take pictures of what the store has so I can tell you which I want. Got it?"

"Got it." She scurried off.

When she came back, she set the selection across my lap – chocolate chip cookie dough, rocky road, Neapolitan, and moose tracks. This wasn't the moment for any fancy shit. I wanted the kind of ice cream I'd eaten as a little kid, and I wanted to gorge myself on it.

I yanked a carton open and stuffed a spoonful into my mouth, not even checking what flavor it was.

Lacey hovered beside the bed. "So… I'm not going to ask, but…"

"Yeah, don't ask."

"All right. I'll be in the hall."

By the sound of her footsteps, she was halfway to the door. Through a mouth full of ice cream, I said, "She fucking dumped me."

Lacey's footsteps re-approached the bed. "We don't have to talk about it if you don't want to."

"Clearly I fucking want to. I just told you what happened."

She was silent for a moment, long enough for me to feel guilty about yelling at her. Before I could apologize, she said, "I'm sorry she dumped you."

Her hand landed on my shoulder, and I gave a little shiver. It'd been so long since anyone had touched me in a friendly way. This woman touched me every day, even bathing me, but always for a reason, never just because.

I liked the way it felt. Liked it a little too much.

"She said I was a downer," I said, desperately hoping she wouldn't take her hand away. "Can you believe that?"

"Well… it's not my place to say."

I wished I could move my neck, because I wanted to whip my head around. "What? Tell me."

"You said you didn't want my opinions of your relationship, so…"

"Now I do."

"You're not going to freak out or get mad at me?"

"No. I promise." *Unless those opinions really make me mad,* I added silently.

"It's just… well…" She gave my shoulder a final squeeze and took her hand off, then sat next to me. "I don't have a whole ton of relationship experience, so take this with a grain of salt. But if someone I loved was suffering… one of my parents or my siblings… I'd do anything I could to be there for them. They wouldn't even have to ask."

"Right."

Briefly, I wondered about her relationship experience. She was definitely attractive, and she clearly had her shit together. I'd pretty much figured she had a husband and kids, even if she was only a little older than me.

"Here's the way I see it," she said. "Tia didn't seem like the best girlfriend to you. If she was, she would've been here every day."

"Yeah, I know."

"Were you two closer before this?" she pushed. "Did you really connect?"

"I don't want to talk about this."

"Okay, I'll go." She got up.

Again, she was halfway to the door when I yelled, "Wait." I shoveled another spoonful of ice cream into my mouth as she came back to me. "No, we didn't really connect. Our conversations were kind of crappy, but the celebrity dating pool is small, especially when you're gay. I thought we were on the same page. That we were both happy with what we had."

"Do you have to date a celebrity?" She set a carton of ice cream that'd fallen over on my lap upright.

"No, but it makes things easier. There's less worry about being taken advantage of."

Except she had taken advantage of me, in a way. She'd ridden my coattails, using our relationship to gain more fame for herself. She had ten times as many Instagram followers now than when we'd started dating. And then the second our situation had required some actual effort from her, she'd thrown me away.

"Let me ask you something," Lacey said. "If it'd

been her who crashed on that ski slope, what would you have done? Would you have gone to visit her?"

"Of course."

She was silent, letting my words sink in.

"Well… I would've visited sometimes." I bit my lip. "At least once, at the start."

"Just like she did."

Okay, she was right. If Tia had crashed and ended up in the hospital, I wouldn't have wanted to put everything else on hold to sit around and hold her hand, either. The rest of my life would've still been going on, and it would've been a lot more fun than the endless wait for bones to heal. I would've wanted to see her in the hospital to make sure she was okay, but after that… I might not have made time to visit.

So, okay, I hadn't been all that invested in the relationship, either. And maybe Tia wasn't a horrible person. Maybe we just hadn't been right for each other.

Or maybe we were both horrible people. That was also possible.

Twelve – Lacey

One would think living in the outskirts of LA would be pretty similar to actually being in the city. One would be wrong. It was more like living in a small town. Everyone knew everyone, and I could barely go to the grocery store without running into someone I'd gone to high school with. Like today.

"Lacey?" The voice came from behind me as I inspected a green apple.

I tensed up, not wanting to talk to anyone. As soon as I turned around, I relaxed. "Lonnie." I set down the apple and went up to him for a hug. "How are you?"

Lonnie had been the only other semi-openly gay person at our high school. After bonding over our sexuality, we'd become inseparable, which had led to most of our class thinking we were secretly dating. We finally officially came out around midway through senior year, and half the class still thought we were just covering up our scandalous relationship.

We'd drifted apart a bit over the past few years. He'd gone to college and actually finished, getting a job that required him to be downtown every day in a suit and tie. I'd been caught up in work and caring for my grandmother, and now that she was gone, I still worked too many hours to hang out with anyone for pleasure.

"I'm great," he said, putting his hands on my shoulders so he could examine me more closely. "You're not, though. You look like a train rolled over you."

I laughed. "Thanks."

"I'm serious. You have giant bags under your eyes – have you been sleeping? You haven't replied to any of the messages I've sent you in forever."

"You might have more luck with that if your messages weren't all jokes about gay sex." I patted his hand, and he released me from his grip. "And I'm sleeping fine," I continued. "Just working too much, but it's a temporary thing."

"How much are you working?"

"About twelve hours a day, six days a week."

His eyes went hazy as he calculated. "Seventy-two hours a week? That's too much for anyone. They're working you to the bone."

"It's only for a little while longer. I'm stockpiling money. Hoping to get back to school."

Zana probably didn't need around-the-clock care anymore – she got around the mansion fine with her crutches. I could've asked her mother's assistant to cut back on my hours now, but somehow I didn't want to – and not just because of the money.

"I'm sure you know what you're doing," Lonnie

said, the concern still evident on his face. "I want you to cut back soon, though, okay?"

"As soon as I can," I lied. "I'll call you when I have some free time. We'll hang out."

"When?"

"A month, month and a half. That's when this gig will be over. All I want to do on my days off right now is sleep."

Lonnie pursed his lips. "Fine." He grabbed my cart.

"Hey!" I followed after him as he headed for the front of the store. "You took my stuff."

"I'm trying to do something nice for you here." He got in line.

"No, no, no." I tugged the cart away from him. "We don't need your charity, but thanks anyway."

*

It was raining as I drove home. My shoes had managed to get soaked in the parking lot, and by the time I got back to my parents' place, all I wanted to do was change into dry socks.

As I brought the groceries in, my dad emerged from his bedroom, sleepy-eyed and pajama-clad. He'd worked the overnight shift, so even though it was mid-afternoon, he was up early.

"Did I wake you? I'm sorry," I said.

"That's okay. Let me get one of those." He pointed at the bag of apples.

I eased into a chair at the table as he crunched into an apple. I hardly got to see Dad, with the amount both of us worked and our opposite schedules.

"You'll never believe what happened," I said. "I ran into an old friend and he offered to buy our groceries for us."

He looked at me sharply. "You didn't let him, did you?"

"Of course not."

"Good. We're not at that stage yet." His mouth formed a hard line. "Which friend was that?"

"Lonnie. Remember him?"

"Ah… nice boy." His eyes softened, and I knew he was remembering all the times Lonnie had come over when we were in high school. "Is he still with that young man he brought over one time?"

"I told you, Dad, they're married now." I'd gone to their wedding back when I was in nursing school. "He's doing well for himself."

I didn't know exactly how much he was making, but clearly it was enough to offer to buy an entire cart of groceries on a whim, not even knowing what the total would be. I'd never understand how money could mean so little to some people. Logically, I knew other people had more of it, so it didn't matter as much. But I fought for every dollar I had, and I didn't spend it without a very good reason.

If I'd had that kind of cash to throw around, I would've fixed the sink in our bathroom, which had been leaky for as long as I could remember. The drip never stopped, so we ended up paying more on the water bill every month.

Mom joined us in the kitchen, and we caught each other up on our lives as Dad went back to bed. I decided not to mention Lonnie and his generous offer. Mom was even more vehemently against taking other people's money than Dad was. This wasn't the first time someone had tried to give us something for nothing, and we always rejected it. The two of them took a lot of pride in being able to support their family.

We talked about Zana instead. Mom was always curious about her, especially about her parents. She was a big fan of both Colette and Maurice King, and of their fairytale relationship.

"I don't know what Zana's mom is like in person," I said. "I haven't met her yet."

"She hasn't come to see her? And her dad only came once?" Mom sounded genuinely shocked. "If you were in that condition, Lacey, I wouldn't leave your side."

"I know you wouldn't." She'd been there for Grandma every single day, doing whatever she could to keep her happy and comfortable. I knew she'd do the same for me if I ever needed her. Still, that was different. "That's why they hired me, so I could be there for her."

"That's not the same." She frowned. "You know, some people have everything, and yet they don't have what really matters."

Was Zana missing what really mattered? She had people in her life who cared about her – didn't she? Her mom had to care, even if she hadn't come to visit. And her dad, although their relationship was clearly strained. She'd had Tia, but that was over now. She did still have friends in her life… although they didn't visit, and she didn't seem to talk to them on the phone.

I wasn't going to feel sorry for Zana. I refused. That brat didn't deserve my pity – she could wipe her tears with hundred-dollar bills.

Still, I had to be grateful for what I had. "Love you," I told my mom.

"Love you, too, Lacey."

THIRTEEN – ZANA

I'm going NUTS! I typed into Twitter. *Anyone broken a bunch of bones before? How'd you deal with it?*

I waited for a minute, expecting responses to pour in. None did, which shouldn't have been a surprise. My tweets were getting less and less attention, probably because they'd turned into a never-ending stream of complaints about being bored.

At least I'd finished wallowing over the break-up. It'd probably hit me again when we went public with it. Tia hadn't posted anything about us not being together, and we still followed each other's social media accounts. I figured she was waiting until I was on my feet again, so she wouldn't have to look like the bad guy.

Out of habit, I clicked over to Google and typed in a Z. The field auto-filled with the rest of my name, and I hit "search."

A news article popped up. *Zana King Spotted Looking Sad In A Taxi.* I clicked it, my jaw already dropping at the stupidity of the headline. Were these people even trying anymore? Why would anyone care about me looking sad in a taxi? There was no story there!

I was used to having no privacy, but usually I

had to at least do something interesting for articles to get written about me. This was a whole other level.

The article talked about my ski crash and how I hadn't been seen in public for weeks. *Zana must be feeling better since she was out and about. Her neck brace is visible in the pics below, so she may not be fully healed.*

Could being stuck at home be the reason for that miserable expression on her face? Her Twitter would say yes, but we suspect it's something deeper. Girlfriend Tia DeSoul has been busy, having been spotted at one of LA's top restaurants the other day, and at a nightclub on the weekend.

Trouble in paradise for one of our favorite couples? We'll keep you updated as soon as we find out!

Great, the paparazzi would be watching me even more than usual. Normally that wouldn't have bothered me, but with my current state of mind, it just made me want to hide out. And just when I'd been hoping I could get out of my place more. Forget that – I'd stay inside another year if I had to.

I clicked back to Twitter. Still no responses to my tweet… but I did have a new email from my mom telling me she was coming to visit. In fifteen minutes.

Seriously, great.

I called Lacey into the room. "My mother's coming, just to warn you. Be prepared."

"Oh!" Her hands flew to her hair, as if a single strand was out of place in her perfect bun. "Colette King is coming *here*? Do I look okay?"

"Chill." I scratched at the edge of my arm cast, trying to get at an itch underneath. "She's coming to see me, not you."

Her face fell. "I know."

I didn't know if she understood what I meant – that my mother cared about very little outside herself – but she was already moving away, bustling around to pick up the few things that needed tidying.

The buzzer sounded a few minutes later, and Lacey went to let her in. From what I could hear of their conversation, Lacey was as starstruck as she'd been with my dad. Bile rose in my throat. I was used to how everyone they met reacted to my parents, but still – it was different with Lacey. She shouldn't have fallen for the act.

She disappeared as Colette came into my room. I guessed she was giving us privacy. Funny, though – for some reason, I wished she hadn't left.

"Hello, sweetheart," Colette said, sitting on the bed in front of me so I'd be forced to look at her. "How are you doing?"

"Been better." I knew the answer I gave didn't matter. Whatever I said, she'd jump straight into talking about whatever she'd come here to talk about.

"Oh, I'm sure. Anyway, I came by to see if you'll be able to attend the Grammys with me next week."

For most of my life, I'd gone along with her and my dad. When I'd been a kid, the media fawned all over our "adorable family." Then I got a bit older and less cute. Once I was eighteen and moved out, I'd stopped going along with them. The performances were cool and all, but overall, it was lame. Half the night was spent waiting for awards to be announced, and if I ever yawned or looked at my watch, the paparazzi would be all over it.

I still went to the after-parties, but not with my parents.

"That's doubtful," I said. "Look at me."

"That's what I'm doing," Colette said. "You look pathetic."

"Uh, thanks."

"The publicity…" She waved a hand as if that'd finish the sentence for her.

And it pretty much did. She thought having me sit with her and Maurice, looking all crippled and pitiful, would be good PR. They'd come off as loving parents who brought me out despite the inconvenience because they didn't want their daughter to miss the biggest night of the year.

The benefit for me would be… well, I didn't see one.

"I don't think so," I said. "I'm supposed to be resting."

"You've been resting for almost three weeks now. You should be halfway healed."

"Fine, I'll be honest. I'd rather stay home."

Colette glared at me. "Do I need to remind you who paid for the caregivers that've been taking care of you all this time?"

I scoffed. *The same person who didn't bother to visit me until she needed something.*

"Okay, we'll do this the hard way. How much do you want?" She pulled her check book out of her purse. "It's one night. A thousand?"

"How about ten?"

She raised an eyebrow. "Five grand, and you're going to look happy and excited the whole time."

"Ten is my final offer if you're going to ask me for a whole night of acting."

"You know what? Fine." She scribbled the amount onto the check and signed it with a flourish. "I'm not going to sit here and squabble. My time is worth more than this."

"Works for me." I reached for the check with my good hand, then sank into the pillows as she got up to leave.

Some families spent time together without any money being exchanged. Simply because they enjoyed each other's company.

But this was my life, and there was no changing it.

Fourteen – Lacey

I stood aside as the stylist who'd come in to do Zana's hair left. Zana's dark roots were still showing, but less than before. Platinum blonde had covered most of the brown. I assumed that was the style these days, because I really had no clue.

Zana's face looked as sulky as usual as she shifted around in her chair. "Could you bring my crutches over? My neck is killing me. I don't think I should've let her tip it back like that while she was washing my hair." She winced as she used the crutches to walk back to the bed.

"Are you excited for tonight?" I asked. "The Grammys?"

She snorted. "No, not really."

I shook my head. It baffled me how she could be so jaded. Even if she'd been to the Grammys before, wouldn't it be an amazing experience every time? Like so much else, she took it for granted.

"I've been there many times," she explained. "They're not fun."

"I doubt that."

"Doubt it all you want. I'm telling you the truth – those awards are bullshit, just like my parents in general." She sighed. "Would you grab me some chips, please?"

"Sure." I went into the kitchen, where the cupboards were stocked with every kind of chip she could want. I tore a bag open so she could reach in with her good hand.

One of her mother's old songs came into my head, and I couldn't help but sing it under my breath as I came back. "Da-da-da, the most beautiful thing I've ever seen… da-da-da, the reason for my life to be…"

Zana's face went pale. "What are you singing that for?"

"It got stuck in my head."

"Well, stop singing it. You know that song's about me when I was a baby, right?"

"Makes sense." I shrugged and went on singing it.

"Seriously, Lacey, *stop*." She leaned forward, shoving her chips aside. I was sure she would've grabbed me if she could've.

"Why does it bother you so much?" I asked, stopping to look straight at her. "Is it that embarrassing?"

"It's not embarrassing. It's a huge fucking joke." Her lip curled back in a way I'd never seen before. "You saw my mom when she stopped by. Do you think she seriously feels that way about me? That song was a load of crap that she put out because it was good for her image. Apparently it still is, considering even you fell for it."

"I'm not going to call you a liar, but…"

Of course her mother adored her. That was what moms did. You couldn't carry a baby for nine months and not bond with it. Besides, that song was heart-wrenching. Colette King wouldn't have sung that for no reason.

I was getting a bit tired of Zana complaining about her parents. Even if they hadn't visited her as much as other people's would've, that was only because they were so busy. Everyone knew how amazing they were and what a wonderful relationship they had. Even someone like me, who didn't follow celebrity gossip, was aware that they were one of the most solid couples in Hollywood. Even my mom knew how great Colette and Maurice King were!

"You think you know more about my life than I do?" Zana's eyes blazed. "That's the thing about being famous. Everyone thinks they know me, and no one fucking does."

"Hey, whoa, chill out. I do know you now. I've spent three weeks getting to know you."

"And yet you still believe a song from twenty years ago rather than what you've seen with your own two eyes." She glared. "How much did my parents visit me, huh? How many times did they even call?"

"They're busy people," I said. "That doesn't mean they don't love you."

"Sure, except they *don't.*" Her voice was rising. "They told me as much when I came out of the closet."

I blinked. "Sorry?"

"You heard me right," she said. "They freaked out, screaming and crying. Not because they thought it was wrong or anything – just because they thought it'd hurt their careers. They wanted me to stay quiet about my sexuality. Tried to bribe me into not talking about it, actually."

There was no way they could've done that... but Zana sure seemed sincere about it.

"I wouldn't take their money," she went on. "I decided being true to myself was more important than making my parents look good. I'd just moved out on my own, so the time was right. They cut me off and disowned me. For a few weeks, we didn't talk."

I could hardly breathe. Was she serious?

"I came out anyway, and what do you know?" she said. "The public reaction was positive, and they realized me being gay was *good* publicity. All of a sudden they wouldn't stop calling me, begging me to do photo shoots and give interviews with them, talking about how we were such a big happy family."

"I... I didn't know any of that. I'm sorry."

"Yeah," she muttered, grabbing the bag of chips. "Not many people do."

I moved away, letting the revelations sink in. I stood at the doorway, watching her shove chips into her mouth. "They must still love you, though," I said. "They're your parents."

"That's very naïve of you to say."

I bristled. How could she of all people call me naïve? But maybe she was right. Not all parents loved their kids, and if I thought otherwise, it was only because I'd lucked out. My family hadn't cared at all when I'd come out, not even my grandparents.

"Sorry," I said again. "I just figured… they pay for all of this for you, don't they? This place?"

"Makes them look good." She took another chip.

"It's just that everything online about your family makes you sound so happy."

"Don't you get it? That's the fucking point!" She pushed on her good hand to turn her whole body to face me. "They pay a lot of money to PR firms to make it look like they're decent people and a happy couple. It's all a sham. They can barely stand each other! The people you think are so great *don't even exist.* They're nothing but stories made up to sell more albums and movies."

My jaw hung open. I had no idea what to say.

"So… I hope that answers your question," she

said flatly. "I'm not excited for the Grammys tonight, and that's why."

*

When Maurice and Colette King arrived in the early afternoon, I greeted them less enthusiastically than before. Now that I was seeing them together, there did seem to be some distance between them I wouldn't have expected. It was nothing they said or did, just a sort of strain in the way they interacted.

I wouldn't have noticed it without Zana's explanation, but since she had, I could see they were putting on a show. And the longer they stayed around me, the more comfortable they became with ditching the act.

"You'll have to get this onto her," Colette told me, thrusting a shimmery gold dress into my hands. "Be sure not to damage it. We have to return it to the designer."

Maurice looked around. "And where's Tia?"

"Tia?" Zana asked, looking aghast.

"Well, of course. We assumed she'd be coming along with us," Colette said breezily.

I frowned. They had some balls acting like Zana's girlfriend was automatically welcome, when they'd reacted the way they had to finding out she was gay. And then, they didn't even know they'd broken up? That'd happened over a week ago. If I'd had a break-up, I would've run straight to my mother.

"Tia and I split up," Zana said. "We just haven't made it public yet."

Her parents exchanged a glance. "Well, that won't do," Colette said. "We need her there tonight. Call her and have her come. We'll pay whatever she wants – to a reasonable extent."

"No way," Zana said. "I don't want her there."

I could see why she didn't. Tia had dumped her. Inviting her would make it seem like Zana still wanted to be with her, and as far as I could tell, that wasn't true.

"Do it," Colette snapped.

"Or what?" Zana scoffed. "Maybe I just won't come at all."

"Then you'd better rip up that check I gave you."

My eyes boggled. Zana's parents were *paying* her to go to the Grammys?

"Fine, whatever," Zana said. "I'll go as long as I don't have to bring a date. But actually, I do want to bring her." She lifted her good arm and pointed her finger straight at me.

My heart nearly stopped. What was she doing?

"Your home care worker?" Colette asked.

"Lacey?" Maurice said at the same time.

"Yeah," Zana said, sounding as if this should've been obvious. "She helps me out a lot. Clearly you have an extra ticket, and if I need to go to the bathroom or something, she can take me instead of you, so you won't have to be disturbed." Sarcasm crept into her voice as she finished speaking.

Both of her parents looked at me as if seeing me for the first time. "It might make us look bad if it seems like we're not taking care of her," Colette said.

It, not *she.* As if I was nothing more than an inconvenient situation for them.

My mouth opened and closed as I searched for words. I wanted to stand up for myself, but I didn't want to go if they didn't want me there. God, it was insane that me going was a possibility at all!

Zana's eyes flicked over to me, then back to her mother. "I've changed my mind," she said. "I don't want to go if Lacey isn't going."

"But... but..." Colette stuttered.

"Which is it?" Zana asked. "Do we both go? Or neither of us?"

Colette's gaze slid back over to me – more specifically, to the agency uniform I had on. "We're going to need to find you something to wear."

Fifteen – Zana

It took us a while to get me dressed. I'd gained a few pounds from lying in bed and eating junk food all the time, so Lacey and I were barely able to cram me into the gold dress Colette had picked.

"Why did you want me to go with you?" she hissed as she tried to yank the zipper up. "This is crazy. Someone like me isn't supposed to be at the Grammys."

"I figured you'd keep me entertained," I said, leaning on a crutch. "And I could see you wanted to go."

Her hands stopped moving. "Are you telling me Zana King did something nice for once?"

"No way." I laughed. "I told you, you're my entertainment for the night."

Once the dress was zipped, we went into my walk-in closet. Lacey was a little sturdier than me, and a lot taller, but I had a few things in mind that might work.

"Try that on," I said, pointing at a black cocktail gown studded with real diamonds. "That one, too." A blue-and-white high-to-low dress with a plunging V-neck.

She frowned at me, but she took the dresses. She

started to step out of the closet, then hesitated. My parents were still out there.

"You can change in front of me," I said. "You've seen me naked often enough. It'd only be fair."

"Or you could go into the other room," she said.

"It's going to take me forever to get out and come back in with these crutches." I smiled lightly. "I promise not to peek."

"Yeah, whatever."

I took that to mean I was allowed to peek. I made no effort to pretend I wasn't looking as Lacey stripped off her black collared uniform shirt, revealing a gray sports bra. I gulped. I'd already known she had a nice body, but the bra was flattening her out. She'd be absolutely voluptuous in a push-up bra – or nothing at all.

She stepped out of her pants, and I nearly had a heart attack. Again, what was beneath her clothes was *way* better than what I'd imagined. Despite her extra pounds, her waist was tiny compared to her full hips, and when she bent to pick up the first dress, I got a good look at her curvaceous rear. Her purple bikini-cut panties clashed horribly with her bra, which made me want to rip them both off her.

I swallowed, leaning on my crutches so I could turn my body and stop looking at her. What was wrong with me? I'd known Lacey was attractive since day one, and I'd never wanted to actually do anything about it – although I hadn't seen her nearly-naked before, either.

"Okay, what do you think?" she asked.

I swiveled back to her. "Oh my God."

"That bad?"

She was wearing the black cocktail gown. It was already form-fitting on me, and on her it was so tight it could've been painted onto her curves. Since she was taller, it hit well above the knee. Her creamy legs went on for miles.

"That *good*," I said.

"I don't feel good about it," she said, surveying herself in the floor-to-ceiling mirrored wall. "I'll try the other one."

I pivoted before I could get hypnotized by her figure again. Too weak to resist the temptation, I only turned partway, so that I could still see half of her reflection in the mirror. I watched her wriggle out of the first dress, my core aching with desire – and it didn't let up even when she'd put on the second dress.

"Wow," I said, staring wide-eyed. "That's… you look…"

This dress had always been too big for me – I'd meant to get rid of it, but hadn't gotten around to it. Now I knew it'd found its true owner. The blue and white silk clung to Lacey's hips, going from her knees on one side to her upper thigh on the other. Oh, and the neckline plunged straight to her navel.

"I feel so exposed," she said, pulling at the neckline as if she could cover herself up. "Do you think I could pin this?"

"No, you need to leave it like that. And to take that sports bra off."

"Is that a rule at the Grammys?" she asked half-jokingly.

"It's my rule."

Something inside me was telling me to take a step forward, to lace my hands around her waist and press my lips to hers. That part of me had clearly forgotten how many of my bones were currently broken, because I wasn't physically capable of doing that.

Where was this coming from, though? Was it just because of seeing her take off her clothes? Or did it have something to do with how she was coming to the Grammys in Tia's place – almost like a date?

I shushed the voice in my mind that'd said that. This wasn't a date at all. She was coming as my care worker, and nothing more. Besides, she was straight, probably married.

She lifted her hand to smooth back a stray hair, and I finally checked. No ring there.

Still – straight. As far as I knew, at least, and when I looked at her closely like this, I did pick up a bit of a vibe. Something about her features, or the set of her eyes… Plus she'd never mentioned a guy, or dating at all.

"All right," she said. "If you're sure, I'll try it without the bra."

"I'm dead positive."

Turning around, she scooted her arms out of the straps, then pulled the bra over her head. When she faced me again, the plunging neckline left little to the imagination. Her body wasn't just great, it was downright incredible.

"That dress was made for you," I said thickly. "You're taking it home with you tonight."

"Oh." Her cheeks going pink, she looked at herself in the mirror again. "As if I'd have anywhere else to wear it."

"Doesn't matter. It belongs to you."

She opened the closet door, and we stepped out together. "Look, we just came out of the closet," she whispered in my ear before my parents took notice of us.

"About time," Colette said. "What took you two so long?"

My heart was thundering too loudly in my ears for me to pay attention. If Lacey had meant what I thought she meant… I might be completely screwed.

Sixteen – Lacey

I was going to the Grammys. I was in a limo, surrounded by a family of celebrities. I'd let my hair down and Zana had done my make-up. My boobs were hanging halfway out of my dress.

Zana fidgeted at my side, seeming as uncomfortable as I felt. Eventually she leaned over and opened the minibar. "Here," she said, handing me a tiny bottle of rum. "You should drink on my behalf, since you say I shouldn't."

I giggled nervously. It was still only four-thirty in the afternoon – apparently the awards ceremony started early and went until late. "I'll take a pass for now."

"I'll have it." Colette took the bottle and threw the whole thing back in one gulp.

"Calm down there," Maurice said. "We don't want a repeat of last year, now, do we?"

I cringed, wishing I could be away from the family drama. I didn't know what had happened last year, but by the sounds of it, I could guess their PR firm had been working overtime.

The limo came to a stop, and I helped Zana out. Only then did I realize we were standing at the edge of a red carpet. Like, a real one – with reporters and photographers encircling us on every side.

"Zana, how are you feeling? When are your casts coming off?"

"Colette, has it been hard to watch Zana recover?"

"Maurice, how did you feel when you heard about Zana's accident?"

Zana hopped forward on her crutches, then paused to look at a reporter. "I'm feeling much better," she told him. "I should be back to normal within a few weeks." She put her good hand on her hip, calmly posing for a picture.

Meanwhile, my heart was pounding in my chest. It'd been nerve-wracking enough to be here at all – now I might be in the news? On TV?

A few feet ahead of us, I recognized a famous country singer. Ahead of her, there was the rapper everyone had been talking about all year. This was crazy! I didn't belong here!

"Who's this with you, Zana?" another reporter called out. "Where's your girlfriend?"

Zana stopped again, and the rest of us stopped with her. "Tia couldn't make it tonight." She put her good hand on my shoulder, causing a flurry of camera flashes and shouted questions.

I stood, frozen. I had no idea what kind of expression was on my face. What was she doing? Was she trying to make it look like I was her date? She was a step ahead of me now, and I hurried to catch up. I was lost enough when I was with her – I'd be completely gone if we got separated.

"Zana, who's your date?" somebody else called. "Colette, Maurice, could you fill us in?"

Before Zana's parents could respond, she hitched herself closer to me and laced her fingers around my wrist. "She's not my date. She's just a friend."

Not her home care worker… a friend?

Did she really see me that way, or was she playing with people's heads?

We got through the rest of the red carpet and found our seats near the front of the Staples Center. Zana had been placed at the end of a row, so she could stick her leg cast into the aisle. I was seated between her and her dad, as if we were a buffer between her and her mother.

As the crowd quieted, the host took the stage. Ian James was a well-known talk show host, and I couldn't believe I was looking at him in person. I reached for my phone, intending to text my mom. I'd left it in the limo, since I didn't have a nice purse. I'd have to wait until afterwards to tell my parents all the crazy things I was about to see.

Ian James announced the first category – Best Regional Roots Music Album. I didn't even know what that meant. Still, I was on the edge of my seat as the nominees were listed and the winner was named.

I stayed on the edge of my seat for about three more awards. Then I whispered to Zana, "How many of these are there?"

"Oh, about seventy," she said. "These are only the pre-awards. See? I *told* you this wasn't going to be fun."

All right, this part of the night might be long and boring. I was still just extremely grateful to be here. I never would've dreamed I'd attend the Grammys, and no matter how long the pre-show was, I wasn't going to complain.

Although by the time two hours had passed, I was having a hard time staying positive. Again, Zana had – surprisingly – been right. "Do you want some food?" I whispered to her. "I saw some waiters handing out hors-d'oeuvres."

"Sure," she said.

I got up, relieved to get out of my seat. If stretching my legs felt this good for me after only two hours, how did it feel for Zana to be in bed all the time? Especially when she'd been so active before? No wonder she was cranky.

I walked around a little, and when I got back with the food, the real show was getting started. I started to hand Zana a slider and a glass of sparkling water, then remembered she could only use one hand. She took the water, and I held the slider to her mouth. We both dissolved in giggles as she bit it in half. Her parents and a few people around us stared at us as if wondering why I would feed her by hand.

Even as I did it, I was wondering the same.

The lights dimmed, and I shoved my own food in my mouth and licked my fingers. The Southwest Corn Dogs burst onto the stage to the opening chords of their latest pop hit, glittery streamers exploding all around them. My ears perked up, and I sat up in my seat. *This* was what I'd come for.

"This is amazing," I whispered to Zana. "I can't believe I'm actually seeing this."

A little smile was on her lips. "I figured you'd like it."

The stage was lit up by different-colored floodlights as Ian James took the mic again, sounding much more enthusiastic as he greeted all the viewers at home. Then they showed a recorded skit from a rapper and an R&B singer that left all of us in stitches.

There was an award. Then a performance. And another award. And another performance.

My boredom was gone, forgotten. I stared at the stage, hypnotized by what I saw. Every so often, overwhelmed by the excitement, I'd say something to Zana. She seemed amused by my starry-eyed wonder, but I didn't let that kill my buzz.

I was vaguely aware that her mom helped her up when she needed the bathroom, and that her dad was the one to get her more food. They were doing my job for me, but none of us seemed to mind. They must've wanted to look good for the cameras, and me – I couldn't think of much beyond the glittering magic in front of me.

All too soon, the night was over, and I tried not to sigh as we left the building.

I'd been like Cinderella tonight, but there would be no repeat of the royal ball.

Seventeen – Zana

My parents dropped us off in the limo, barely saying goodbye – probably anxious to each get back to their separate lovers. My mom had a boyfriend she'd been secretly seeing for at least a few years now, and my dad had different women in his bed every night of the week. Their infidelity used to bother me. Tonight, I didn't care.

At my place, Lacey wrapped me in a hug, and then she was off, too. I wished she'd stay longer, but I was too caught up in that intoxicating, uniquely Lacey scent to even think.

My overnight caregiver lay on the sofa, waking from her nap as I clomped through the living room. "You're back from the Grammys," she said. "How was it?"

"Good," I said simply.

If I liked her as much as Lacey, I'd tell her how it'd been so much better than other years. How seeing Lacey's childlike excitement had given me a renewed interest in the repetitive proceedings. How having her there to talk would've made even the worst torture feel like nothing.

But I didn't like her as much as Lacey. I didn't like many people that much.

I got my own glass of water and scooted into bed, still thinking about how awed Lacey had been. She was always so stoic, so rarely showing emotions. At the ceremony, she'd looked like she was in a dream. The huge smile had never left her face, and with her make-up and hair – not to mention that *cleavage* – she'd looked more gorgeous than I'd ever seen her.

With a sigh, I reached for my tablet. I wanted to see some of the media coverage from tonight. I wasn't sure exactly what I was looking for, but it didn't take me long to find it.

Zana King Flirts With Mystery Woman At Grammys – Tia DeSoul Left In The Dust?

My heart sank as I clicked the article. They'd been thorough, all right. There were the pictures of me and Lacey from before the pre-show – the ones on the red carpet where I'd been touching her. Then, as I scrolled, there was a video of her feeding me, and one of me looking at her affectionately as she watched a performance.

The text was all about how no one knew who Lacey was, and I'd "mysteriously" referred to her as "a friend." The comments speculated that she was an Instagram model, but no one had been able to find her profile – and apparently a lot of people had looked. They all thought I'd cheated on Tia with her, and they were furious about it.

"Holy shit," I murmured to myself. People needed to get a grip and stop making assumptions before they knew anything about anything.

As I looked at the comments, someone posted a screenshot from Tia's Twitter. *Sorry to say, I have nothing to say about anything that happened at the Grammys tonight,* she'd written. *I wasn't invited, and I don't know anything more than that.*

Technically that was true, but she had some nerve to twist things and make them look like she was the victim here. *She'd* dumped *me!* Briefly, I considered writing a tweet – or ten – and explaining things for myself. But at the moment, I couldn't be bothered.

Let those no-life Internet commenters send themselves into a tizzy over something that in no way affected them. Let Tia try her best to boost her own reputation by bringing me down.

For now, all I wanted to do was sleep – and hopefully dream of the joyous look that had been on Lacey's face.

*

"Morning, sleepyhead." Lacey was sitting on the edge of my bed as I slowly opened my eyes.

I felt so tired, as if I was hung over, but I hadn't had anything to drink. Just staying up late after sleeping all the time for three weeks must've knocked me out.

"Morning," I said. "You have a good time last night?"

She helped me sit up straight. "Amazing," she said. "My family kept me up half the night asking me about what I saw."

"Tell me you didn't Google it."

"No," she said sharply. "Why?"

"Nothing. Mind helping me to the bathroom?"

She made a face, but said nothing as she helped me get on my feet. Sparks leapt through me where she touched me, and I tried my best not to moan. I was definitely developing a crush – a ridiculous, idiotic crush.

Once I was alone, I splashed my face with my good hand. How would dating Lacey even work? First I'd have to assume she was gay or bi, which was still unclear. Then there was the whole matter of the terrible first impression I'd made – and the entire three weeks that'd come after it.

She'd never go for me after the way I'd treated her. Not if I was the last person on Earth.

I brushed my teeth, careful not to move my head. Even if some miracle occurred and she did like me, what then? She wasn't famous. Was I supposed to bring her into my world? I was pretty sure I could trust that she wouldn't be after my money, but how would she ever fit in if she was always as starstruck as she'd been last night? As much as she acted like she had such a no-nonsense attitude, it all went out the window when she encountered any celebrities other than me.

Well, that meant she was comfortable with me. That was a good first step.

I clomped out of the bathroom and over to the bed, where Lacey had already set up my breakfast tray.

She had her phone in her hand, and her face was pale as she looked up at me. "The whole world thinks we're dating? Why would you want people to think this?"

"Whoa, it's not like I planned it this way. I only wanted you to come in a work capacity. I guess our body language said otherwise."

She shook her head. "Didn't you see it could look that way? Do you still not see how this could affect people other than you? If my agency catches wind of this, I'll be out of a job!"

"Okay, chill out. I'll hop on Twitter and clarify. There'll be a million Buzzfeed articles about it within the hour. Everyone will feel bad about jumping to conclusions, and the whole thing will be old news by the time you're done work today."

Her face softened. "Are you sure?"

"Totally sure." I eased myself onto the bed and grabbed my tablet. "I'll clear everything up, don't you worry." I rapidly tapped out a series of tweets.

1. Very disappointed in the assumptions that are being made about me. Time to set the record straight. First of all, Tia dumped me. Apparently dealing with an injured girlfriend is too much of a drag for her.

2. Second, the woman who was with me at the Grammys was my home care worker. Is she gorgeous? Yes. Am I lucky enough to be dating her? No. She was there in a work capacity, and that's all.

3. So check yourselves before you start talking about things you have NO idea about.

4. I don't actually care what you have to say about me, but leave her out of this. Just – leave her out of it.

I handed the tablet to Lacey. She read silently, except for a sharp intake of breath.

"You… said you'd be lucky to date me?" she asked in a tight voice.

"Oh." Maybe I should've read over what I wrote before posting it. "I mean, you know, well…"

She blinked, and then blinked again. "Huh?"

"Never mind." I sighed. Of course dating her would never work. I'd be a fool to even think about it. "I'll edit the tweet."

EIGHTEEN – LACEY

"Hey there, famous lady!" Lonnie's voice came cheerily through the phone. "I've been trying to reach you for days. Guess you're too busy being famous to pick up a call."

I'd just gotten home from Zana's, and I yawned as I dropped my purse on the kitchen table. My entire body was exhausted, and all I wanted was to sink into bed. "Not famous. Just busy."

"Sure, because non-celebrities always have article after article analyzing their appearance at the Grammys." He scoffed. "I still haven't forgiven you for not inviting me, by the way. You can make it up to me by taking me next year."

"Next year? This was a one-time thing. What are you even talking about?"

"Do you think the entire world hasn't seen Zana's original tweet? We all know she said she'd be lucky to date you, so you'll be her plus-one next year, and you can take me as your guest!"

For the past couple of days, I'd been trying my best to avoid the constant analysis of Zana's tweets online. It should've been easy since I didn't follow celebrity gossip, but sometimes morbid curiosity made me check out the articles and Twitter threads.

It seemed that a lot of people out there doubted the truth of what Zana had said. Although Zana had changed her tweet within minutes, the Internet had noticed what it'd originally said, and the edit had made a lot of people suspicious about what might be going on between us.

They were convinced she'd been cheating on Tia, and they were full of bitter vitriol – not for her, but for me. Apparently she and Tia were "couple goals," and I was nothing but a hussy and a homewrecker.

I tried to let the harsh words roll off my back, but honestly, it hurt to read those things. I hadn't done anything wrong, and I definitely hadn't broken up Zana's relationship. Why were people so eager to hate me? They'd latched onto the smallest reason to create a vendetta against someone they'd never met. Did they have nothing happening in their own lives?

A small segment of people thought I was cute. I'd been dubbed "Home Care Bae," and they talked about how they'd break all their bones if I'd be the one to take care of them. Maybe I should've been flattered, but in actuality, that attention only made me feel weird. Those people didn't know me, either.

Besides, I'd only looked good because of the make-up and the dress that had half my chest hanging out. If those people saw me in my normal uniform, they'd never look at me twice.

So far, my agency hadn't said anything to me, and I prayed it'd stay that way. As long as I could claim I'd only been at the Grammys in a professional capacity, I'd be fine.

"I'm not going to date Zana," I said.

"Why not? Are you telling me you're not into her?"

"Yes, that's exactly what I'm saying."

Lonnie snorted. "That's not what I got from the pictures. You two were looking pretty damn cozy. You know a picture says a thousand words, and those ones were screaming you were into each other."

"Cut it out. They weren't."

"Of course they were. Why do you think the entire world thought you were on a date?" I could practically hear his eyes rolling. "You were *feeding* her, for God's sake!"

"She has a broken arm!"

"Stay in denial as long as you want. Somewhere in that stubborn ol' brain of yours, you know I'm right." He barely paused before shifting topics. "Anyway, when are we going to hang out? I haven't seen you in forever."

"I know, and I miss you, but this job is sucking the life out of me. I have zero time outside of work. My days off are taken up by laundry and sleep."

"It can't be that hard to spend all of your days

with a girl you're secretly in love with."

"Secretly *what?*"

He laughed uproariously. "Why don't you invite me by her place? I'd like to meet your future wife. And all of her celebrity friends."

"Okay, you're just pushing my buttons now," I muttered. "You're ridiculous."

"Yeah, maybe." He stopped laughing, and his voice got serious. "For real, Lacey, do what makes you happy. Life is too short for anything else."

My throat felt tight. "I'm as happy as I'm going to be. I don't have secret feelings for Zana, so forget about that."

"Whatever you say."

*

When I got to Zana's place the next day, I was surprised to find her in the armchair in the living room. She usually slept until well after my arrival.

"C'mon, let's get going," she said. "Shower time. I'm dying to get out of the house."

A thrill went through me at the thought of seeing her naked again. I immediately chastised myself. I was *not* supposed to have dirty thoughts about my clients. I was a professional, not some kind of pervert.

"Sure," I said, helping her onto her crutches.

She hurried into the bathroom, and I got the shower running. I knew she liked her water close to boiling, so I put on her cast covers while it got sufficiently hot.

"Why do you want to get out so bad?" I asked. "Going stir-crazy?"

"Exactly. I've been cooped up for ages. It wasn't so bad until we went to the Grammys and I remembered there's a whole world out there I've been missing."

With the cast covers on, I checked the water. It was hot. "So what do you want to do?" I took a deep breath and pulled off her nightgown, trying not to show the effect her nudity had on me.

Her body was the same as it'd always been – that is to say, absolutely gorgeous. It'd never bothered me before, even knowing she was gay, even after she became single. But now that she'd made that accidental comment about liking me, things had changed.

She seemed attainable now – even if I'd never wanted to "attain" her before. We were from different worlds, and I was fine with that! I wasn't interested in her, even if she was interested in me, which obviously she wasn't.

Yes, she was beautiful. I had eyes and a pulse. I would've had to be blind and/or dead to not notice her beauty. But that wasn't all I needed in a partner. Besides, I wasn't looking for a partner! Where would I find time to date?

A little voice in my head reminded me that I spent all day, every day with Zana already...

But as soon as this assignment is over, I'll have a new client, so shut up!

I helped Zana onto the chair inside the shower. Doing my best to keep out of the water, I soaped up the areas she couldn't reach with her good hand. I kept my eyes off her glimmering breasts, doing my best to look at her as little as I could. Still, I couldn't ignore the way her skin felt soft and sleek beneath my fingers.

"Mmm," she moaned as I rubbed shampoo into her hair.

Okay, that was enough. I couldn't suppress the thoughts going through my head anymore – not when she was wet and naked in front of me. I ducked out of the shower and stood with my back against the wall, trying futilely to catch my breath.

"Let me know when you're done," I called.

By the time she turned the water off, I'd somewhat recovered – but that only lasted until I had to help her onto her crutches and towel her down. Every drop of water gleaming from her smooth skin tempted me, and the smell of her jasmine bodywash was tantalizing.

My hormones were going out of control. *She's*

been awful to you, I reminded myself. *She's been a huge jerk since day one.*

Except for how she'd taken me to the Grammys for no other reason but because she could see I wanted to... that'd been pretty damn nice.

I hung up the towel and wrapped a bathrobe around her. "Let's something for you to wear," I said. "Where do you want to go, anyway?"

"To the beach." She sighed.

I glanced at her casts and crutches. "Not likely. Where else?"

"Shopping, maybe? Rodeo Drive?"

The area of town where every item cost as much as my family's rent for a month. "Sure," I said.

Nineteen – Zana

I should've known. Seriously, I should've known. I must've been stupid to think I could have a nice afternoon out with Lacey and get away with it.

Well, the "nice afternoon" part had gone fine. We'd shopped for a few hours, and despite how hard it was for me to get around, I'd been in her company, so it'd been fun. We joked and laughed as we picked through furniture and housewares for my place. We even stopped for lunch, and the conversation hadn't even faltered. It felt an awful lot like being out with a friend… or a girlfriend.

I felt strange about dragging her to those expensive stores where she'd never afford to buy anything, so after lunch, I took her to a jewelry store. I'd noticed her watch when we first met, and not in a good way. It looked like a ten-dollar watch from the sales rack at Target. Not only was it cheaply constructed, it was also twice as big as her wrist, and she was constantly pushing it up when she needed to check it.

"Pick one," I said, gesturing at the display case of infinitely nicer watches.

"What?" She snapped around to look at me. "I have a watch."

"An awful one. I'm getting you a new one."

"I like mine." She covered it with her hand.

"You'll like your new one better, so hurry up and pick one."

Eventually she gave in and chose a gorgeous silver one with delicate interlocking links. It made me happy to see it on her wrist, and even happier when she let me throw the old one in the garbage.

Now, though, she'd gone home, and I was Googling myself as the overnight care worker napped in the other room. Apparently the paparazzi had spotted us today, and the public still hadn't learned to not jump to conclusions.

Zana King Spotted Spoiling Potential New Love Interest, one article read.

It went on to talk about how I'd been seen with Lacey on Rodeo Drive, and how even though she'd been in her work uniform, it was pretty obvious that there was something between us. Even I had to admit the picture of us walking out of the jewelry store, her hand on my arm, looked romantic.

It wasn't, though. And now she was going to get mad again – and she'd be right. I shouldn't have taken her out when I knew that misinterpretations like this could mess up her career. All I'd wanted was to get out of the house – but I'd only been thinking about myself. As usual.

The door buzzed, and I frowned. I needed to buzz to let visitors in unless they had the entry code, which no one did, except... Lacey.

I sat up straight as the front door opened and her heels clopped on the floor. She didn't bother to take her shoes off, instead coming straight toward me. When she positioned herself in my sightline, I saw the look of fury on her face.

"What were you *thinking?*" she asked, jamming her phone in my direction. "Did you *know* how today was going to look?"

"No!" I said, trying to sound vehement when I was really drinking the sight of her in. She looked hot when she was mad.

"Well, it got me fucking *fired!*"

Never mind looking hot. Her anger was terrifying. "What?"

She nodded, her lips forming a thin line. "Someone at the agency saw the articles about today. Apparently they'd been aware of the publicity I got at the Grammys and were 'monitoring the situation.' They aren't happy with how I made the agency look, especially since I was wearing their uniform shirt while I was supposedly breaking their code of conduct."

"But you didn't do anything." I hated to see her this upset. I had to find a way to make it right. "What's the agency's number? I'll call and tell them we weren't up to anything. They'll listen to me. They'll have to."

"No, they won't!" She interrupted before I was finished speaking. "They're sending the new care worker in tomorrow. This is the last time you're going to see me, Zana."

Well, shit. My mouth hung open and I stared at her as she fumbled the watch off her wrist.

"And you can have this back," she said. "I don't want it."

"Don't say that. It was a gift for you. Please." I pushed it back at her. "Consider it a leaving bonus, if you really have to leave. I – I don't want you to."

I hated the thought of some new care worker coming in the door in the morning. Working out a new routine, getting used to each other's quirks. Spending the whole day with someone else. Someone who wasn't Lacey.

I wouldn't have minded the idea so much if Lacey could still be in my life in some other way. If we could stay in touch… stay friends… But no, she'd said this was the last time I'd see her. We weren't even leaving on good terms – she was upset with me, and for good reason.

"I don't want to leave either, but what else can I do?" Her eyes shone. "I'm going to have to find a new job. The agency isn't going to give me any more assignments, and any other employers are going to find out about this mess during background checks."

My mind raced. What if I offered her a job? I could spare the money to hire a personal assistant or a secretary, even if I didn't really need one. No, she wouldn't fall for that. She had way too much pride to take my money like that.

Besides, I didn't want her around in a "professional capacity." I wanted her here because she wanted to be. Because she enjoyed my company and wanted to see me.

But did she?

My heart in my throat, I took her hand with my good one. "You'll figure something out. I know you will. You're too smart and industrious to go without work for long."

Her gaze snapped to our joined hands. "Zana…"

"I want to see you again," I said softly. "I'll understand if you're not interested. I'm not even sure if you swing that way. But if there's any chance…"

She dropped my hand. "What are you asking?"

"Look, I don't want to make you uncomfortable. This is your job – or was." I leaned forward, praying she'd understand. "There's a reason all those news articles think there's something between us. For me, there is. And I think – I hope – you feel it, too."

"Why would you have feelings for me?" Her voice broke. "It doesn't make sense."

"Because you're beautiful, to start off." I bit my lip. "Because you're real and you don't sugarcoat things for me. You treat me like a normal person, and you don't give a fuck if I'm famous."

"Anyone could do that."

"Not like you do." My pulse raced faster and faster. "You're not like anyone else, Lacey. I can talk to you about nothing for hours without getting bored. I can spend a whole day with you and still want more. You make me laugh. You make me think. You *get* me, and that's rare."

She stared into my eyes, still standing close enough that I could feel her breath on my skin. "I want – I can't – "

"Forget the can't," I breathed. "Focus on the want."

Her tongue darted out and she licked her lips quickly, her eyes searching mine as she made her decision. That millisecond felt like an hour. Would she kiss me, or back away completely? It felt like my entire future hung in the balance, like this action would have consequences that reverberated for years.

Finally she leaned in, time still moving in slow motion. She was going to kiss me… going to kiss me… my mind struggled to believe it, and then her lips were on mine, as soft and sensuous as I ever could've imagined. She was on the bed, her arms wrapping around me, and my good hand lifted so I could run my fingers through her hair.

Kissing her could've healed every broken bone in my body, right then and there. Being here with her – her hands on me, her delicate scent in my nostrils – made everything better. All was right with the world, if only for a few seconds.

And then she pulled away. She looked into my eyes, her breath audible and ragged. She'd realized she made a mistake – she was going to say we had to stop...

But all she said was, "Did I hurt you?" She brushed a finger over my neck brace.

"Not at all."

I pulled her in again, feeling every part of my body respond to her as waves of relief and gratitude flooded over me. She didn't regret kissing me, at least not yet. She was doing it again, and that meant there might be more kisses in the future, or even more than that.

And that prospect was more thrilling than it should've been. I'd been with my fair share of women before – not a ton, actually, but I'd had a few girlfriends. Lacey was just so different from any of them. She was real and genuine and she didn't hold back. What would she be like in bed?

Footsteps at the door made us snap apart. "I didn't realize you had a guest," the overnight care worker said sleepily. "Don't mind me. I'll be back in the living room."

"That's probably my cue to go," Lacey said,

extracting herself from my one-armed embrace

"No, stay." I clung to her as she stood up.

"I need some time to think." She smiled apologetically. "I wasn't expecting… well, any of this."

"Tell me we can go on a date soon," I said. "A proper date."

Slowly, she nodded. "I'd like that. We're going to set some ground rules, though. No ordering me around. No being a jerk."

"I'll try my best."

TWENTY – LACEY

What did I wear for a date with someone I had no earthly reason to go out with? I brushed my hair roughly as I looked through my closet. Zana had never seen me in my own clothes, only the agency uniform and, that one time, her own dress. What would she be into? And why did I care?

I had clearly gone crazy for agreeing to this date in the first place. I didn't even *like* Zana, for heaven's sake! She infuriated me on a regular basis. She was spoiled and selfish and entitled, and… I couldn't get her out of my mind.

Grabbing ripped jeans and a cropped sweater, I threw them onto my bed. I wasn't going to worry about what kind of underwear I had on. Clearly our date wasn't going to go that far. I doubted sex would even be possible, with the condition she was in – although then again, she did have one good arm…

No. I had to stop thinking that way. I should call her now and cancel this date. It made no sense to go. None.

I could admit she wasn't *as* bad as she'd been when I'd met her. I'd definitely gotten used to her, to an extent. But liking her as a patient wasn't the same as liking her romantically!

She'd given me a bunch of reasons that she liked me, but could I say any of the same for her? Okay, I enjoyed her company. It'd been surprisingly fun to binge-watch TV together. Did she *get* me, though? I had to say no. Not at all.

And then there was the fact that the world already thought we were dating – and they hated me for it. There was no way we'd get away with going out in public together without a photographer spotting us. Tomorrow's news would be full of more mean articles about me. Why was I opening myself up to more vitriol?

I glanced at my watch – the new one she'd given me. I had to cancel or get going – and for some inexplicable reason, I couldn't convince myself to cancel.

Twenty minutes later, I pulled up in front of the restaurant she'd told me to come to. I wasn't sure how she thought we were going to get away with this without the paparazzi taking note, and I was already worried. I'd been applying to jobs for the past three days straight, and I didn't need any more scandals to decrease my chances even further.

When I stepped inside, a black-coated waiter greeted me, seeming to already know who I was. "Ms. Howard, follow me."

He led me through the room, and I noticed the other tables were empty. Zana sat at the back, accompanied by a man I didn't recognize. He helped her out of her seat, and she gave me a tight hug with her good arm.

"Who's this?" I asked, giving the stranger a skeptical look.

"My new care worker, Jason." She eased herself back into her seat. "He's not chaperoning us or anything. I just wanted to make sure you wouldn't have to do anything that seemed even slightly work-related. I'd like you to forget you ever worked for me."

That was actually incredibly considerate. "I'll try," I said. "I'm guessing you had something to do with this place being empty, too?"

"I asked them to let us have the place for the afternoon." She smiled. "We're having a private party, even if it only happens to be three people."

"Two, really." Jason got up. "I'll be over here reading the newspaper. Just give me a shout if you need anything, Zana."

"Sounds good, and you order whatever you want."

Now we were alone, and a shiver came over me as I looked at her. I was seriously on a date with Zana King. How much had she paid to get the whole restaurant to ourselves? I tried to tell myself it didn't matter, that she had enough money to do whatever she wanted with it – but I couldn't shake the feeling that she'd paid something in the range of my food budget for a month.

"So…" she said, toying with the edge of the menu. "How've you been?"

"Not bad," I said. "You?"

"Good." She picked the menu up, and I could tell she was trying to get it in front of her face, but it was too bulky. She wasn't going to be able to, and I wasn't going to help. "Jason, if you could?"

Jason rushed over, but the waiter got to us first. "I can tell you the specials for the day, madam."

Without looking at the menu, we all agreed to take the special – risotto with braised chicken and harvest vegetables. The food was the last thing on my mind, and I suspected Zana felt the same.

Once the waiter was gone, she set her good elbow on the table. "Where were we? Oh yes… So, are you gay, or what?"

I nearly choked on thin air. "Um…"

"Okay, that's not where we were, but I've been dying to know ever since we kissed. Was that just to try it, or…?"

"No, I'm gay. Pretty freaking gay."

She looked relieved. "Cool. Uh, same."

"I'm aware."

It hit me again how uneven our relationship was so far. I knew everything about her, and she knew nothing about me. *I don't need your entire life story,* she'd told me – but that'd been the first day, when she'd been in a ton of pain.

Besides, I might not know as much about her as I thought. I'd already learned how information could get twisted before it made its way to the public. Even things I knew from being around her had turned out to be dead wrong.

We both had a lot of learning to do – if this was going to go anywhere, that was.

The waiter returned with our risotto, along with a glass of wine for each of us. I took a generous sip, hoping that'd calm my nerves. I was out of my element here, and there was no guidebook for this situation. Or was there? I made a mental note to Google "how to date a celebrity you originally hated" when I got home.

I took a bite of the food and closed my eyes. "Mmm, this is scrumptious!"

"Right? I love this place. They make the best risotto in LA."

"Oh, there's better risotto outside LA?"

"I mean, nothing compares to the real stuff you get in Italy." She shrugged.

Another twinge of apprehension went through me. I'd never been to Italy – never even left the US. How could this ever work?

"I'll have to try it sometime," I said stiffly.

"Maybe I'll take you one day." She put her hand

over mine. "I'm so glad you're gay. Makes this much easier."

"Why, you were planning to seduce me even if I was straight?"

She looked guilty. "It did cross my mind." She tried and failed to cut her chicken one-handed. "Jason?"

He rushed over to help, which gave me time to get the blush off my face. I waited for him to leave before speaking again. "I actually haven't dated much. I generally don't have time for things like that."

"Not much, as in…?"

"Never," I clarified. "I mean, I've had a date here and there." There was one time I'd met a girl at a house party, and once a friend had set me up on a blind date. "They just haven't gone anywhere."

"Ah." She sipped her wine. "I never had that problem."

"Well, I guess you have more free time for dating than I do." I tried not to sound catty. I had to accept Zana as she was for this relationship to have any chance of working out – something I was starting to seriously hope would happen.

"I'm like Kiara from *Doctor Files*, basically," she said.

I had to smile. "I still can't believe we powered

through fifteen seasons."

"I just wish there were fifteen more," she said. "Want to start over?"

"Maybe we could start on another show first." I speared a piece of broccoli, trying not to look at Zana. "I've been hearing good things about *Unheard Music.*"

"Never heard of it," she said. "But I'll watch it with you."

She was being sweet again, and I didn't know what to think. I liked this side of her... but I'd seen another side, too, and I wasn't sure which was the real her.

What if they both were? Would I be able to handle that?

TWENTY-ONE – ZANA

When dinner was over, the waiter cleared away our plates. "Stay as long as you like," he told us. "You have the run of the place for the rest of the evening."

The idea was tempting. Staying here talking with Lacey until the sun went down and came back up? I couldn't think of many things I'd like better.

But there was one other thing, and if she happened to be in the mood for it, I definitely wanted it more than talking.

"Do you want to come back to my place?" I asked innocently. "We could check out *Unheard Music*."

Her eyes searched mine, and I could tell she'd seen right through the flimsy cover story. She opened her mouth, then closed it and bit her lip. "Are you sure you're up for watching that?" she finally asked. "From what I've heard about that show, it might be tough to watch in your condition."

"Why would it be tough?" I asked, widening my eyes at her. "I'll just be lying there watching it." Wait, did that sound like I didn't want to do anything to her? Because I did, I definitely did. "I mean, aside from when you're watching it."

A smile crept across her face. "Wouldn't we both be watching it, anyway? Isn't that the point?"

I stared at her. "Okay, I'm confused. What are you talking about?"

"TV, of course. Why? Did you mean something else?"

If I could've shaken my head, I would've. "No more games. You're coming home with me."

"Yes, ma'am."

Jason drove us back, and he was smart enough to realize we needed some privacy. "I'll be in the guest room. Ring the bell if you need anything."

"Actually, I think you'll be better off downstairs," I said. "I'll call your phone if I need you."

He cleared out, and Lacey and I were alone – the way we'd been every day for three weeks straight, and yet it felt completely different this time around.

She hurried around the room, turning the lights off and the TV on while I clambered into bed. I left space for her to sit beside me on my left, and when she climbed in next to me, I dared to put my good hand on her thigh.

A little gasp came out of her, and I worried I'd done too much, too soon – but then her fingers laced through mine, and both of our breathing settled as the first episode of the show came on.

We watched for about three minutes, and then I squeezed her thigh gently, and then she climbed on top of me, straddling me as she kissed me again. My mind swirled as her lips brushed mine. This felt even better than it had before, maybe because I knew it wasn't a fluke this time. She *wanted* to kiss me, and if she was doing it twice, that might mean she'd do it again and again.

Her hands crept down to my waist, and we both sighed out loud as skin met skin. A fire was starting in my core, burning for her to touch me *everywhere.* And I wanted to touch her just as much. I wasn't sure how much I'd be able to do to her with my one arm, but I certainly planned to try.

I ran my left hand along her cheek, then down her neck and along her shoulder. She'd left her hair down today, and the fine strands grazed my fingers, raising goosebumps all over me. I looked her in the eye, and the eagerness there told me not to stop. I caressed her breasts, stoking the fire inside me higher.

"I know I promised you wouldn't have to help me anymore," I whispered, "but I don't really want to call Jason here to take your clothes off. Would you mind?"

Her cheeks went pink. "I'm not going to make you do anything to me. You're not physically capable."

"I wouldn't mind if you sat on my face and

broke my neck all over again," I said. "At least it'd be more fun than the last time. But for the moment, this arm does work, and I'm more than ready to use it."

Her blush intensified. "I guess I can't say no to that."

She took off her clothes outside my line of vision, but as I sat there with the brace holding my head straight forward, I didn't care that I couldn't see her. As soon as she sat beside me, I could *feel* her – her softness, her wetness – and I could hear the little moans that emerged from her as I found my way around her center.

I wished I could use my right hand... I wished I could use my *tongue*... but for now, I was grateful to just be here with the woman I'd wanted for weeks. I moved my hand in small circles until her hips bucked harder and harder.

Her breath came in shallow gasps. "Oh, fuck, Zana..."

I loved how she moaned my name. I wanted to hear her moan it again – and again. And I wasn't going to let a few broken bones stop me from drawing it out of her.

Eventually she pushed my hand away and wriggled between my legs. She'd taken my pants off so many times before that my hips lifted automatically. This time, what came after was something else entirely.

She held my hips as she made her way between

them. Her tongue brushed against my aching spot, and a jolt of pleasure went through my body. The pleasure intensified as she went on, diving deeper into my center. All the pain and the injuries melted away. All I knew was the bliss of being completely and utterly cared for.

The first orgasm was world-shattering. The second just built on that. And the ones after that were even better. I had no idea how much time passed as Lacey coaxed climax after climax out of me. It felt like an eternity, because by the time I finally couldn't take anymore, I couldn't remember what my life had been before she put that tongue on me, and I had no idea what would happen after.

As I slowly returned to the present, my mind calmed and I found that I was able to think again. And the only thing I wanted to think about was how to keep Lacey's warmth next to me as I fell asleep.

"Stay with me," I murmured sleepily. "Stay the night."

She pulled the sheets over both of us and snuggled up beside me. "What's Jason going to think?"

I put my good arm over her, enthralled by the softness of her skin. "He'll be absolutely scandalized."

TWENTY-TWO - LACEY

I woke up blurrily, unsure of where I was. It took me a few minutes to put the pieces together, one after another. Working for Zana… getting fired… Zana asking me out… and then… last night.

My breath caught in my throat as I realized I was still here, in her bed. Sparks leapt through me as memories of the intimacy we'd shared raced through my brain. It'd been everything I could've wanted in a first time, and it'd been with the girl the entire world wanted.

I took a moment to appreciate the absurdity of it all. That a sex symbol like Zana had chosen *me*, and that I'd been so resistant to being with her.

Now – well, now I didn't know what happened next. We'd been on one date and had sex. One date and sex didn't make her my girlfriend, although she hadn't acted like this was some casual fling either. But how could it be more than that? How could an internationally known celebrity like her wind up with someone like me?

Just the rumors of us dating had made a mess of my life. Now they could potentially become true. What would my parents think?

Oh, God. What were my parents thinking right

now? I'd never stayed out all night before. I grabbed my phone and checked the time. If I left this instant, I might be able to get home before my dad got back from work. What about my mom, though? She'd be up by now, and she'd have no idea where I was.

"Zana!" I shook her shoulder, positioning myself in her sightline. "Zana, I have to get going."

Her eyes blinked open, and she looked up at me sleepily. "Lacey... Don't go."

"I have to." I jumped up and searched for my clothes, scattered here and there on the floor. "My mom's gotta be freaking out. I'll call you later."

"Or you could call her now."

I froze where I stood. "That's... true."

"She knows you were on a date last night, right?" she asked. "She can probably put two and two together, and even if she couldn't, calling would set her mind at ease."

"Yeah, sure, but..." But I didn't necessarily want my mom to know I'd – finally – gotten laid. Then again, it might be a bit late for that... and the idea of sleeping in late with Zana did sound appealing. "Okay, I'll call."

A quick, awkward phone call later, and I was back in bed. She was already fast asleep.

All the panic had gotten me way too worked up

to follow her lead. I lay awake, playing through different scenarios of how this could go in my mind until at last she woke up again.

"How'd you sleep, beautiful?" She reached for my hand.

"Less than amazingly." I let her hold my hand, but didn't return the squeeze she gave it. "What are we doing here, Zana? I'm not up for some casual fling."

She heaved herself upward until she was sitting next to me, back against the headboard like usual. "Did I say I wanted a fling?"

My voice went small. "You didn't say much about what you wanted." And I'd slept with her anyway, which was completely unlike me. I'd always thought my first time would be after dating for a while, maybe even saying "I love you."

"I've only known you for a few weeks, but I know I like you." She twisted her body toward me. "I'd like to see how things go."

"That sounds good." She didn't sound quite as certain as I would've wanted – but then, I wasn't certain, either. "Let's hope the paparazzi don't catch wind of it."

"God!" She huffed out a laugh. "Can you imagine?"

*

It took less than a day for the paparazzi to catch wind of it.

I finally left Zana's place around six that night, feeling the need to get home and make dinner for my mom. Now that I wasn't working, I could get home before nine-thirty and take some of the load off her, for once. She normally started dinner the second she got back from work, and she hardly ever got a break.

As soon as I walked out of Zana's door, a camera flash temporarily blinded me. I rubbed my eyes, confused, and then I realized what'd happened.

I called her to warn her during my drive back. By the time I got home, she'd sent me a news article about my "walk of shame."

Lacey Howard was spotted leaving Zana King's home in the same clothes she was wearing the night before – and not the uniform she used to wear, either. Could things be heating up between these two ladies? We can't say for sure, but we do know this – we feel sorry for Tia DeSoul. It must be hard to see her ex moving on so fast.

My stomach roiled as I sat parked in my driveway reading the article. I hadn't done anything to deserve anyone's attention! Why did the general public care where I spent the night? Even though the article hadn't said any specifically bad things about me, I didn't like that they were paying attention to me at all.

I wasn't interesting. My private life wasn't anyone's business. I was just like anybody else.

The injustice of it all rankled for a long moment before it finally hit me.

This was how Zana had felt all her life.

Twenty-Three – Zana

So Lacey and I were in the public eye. That was a bit awkward for me. Probably worse for her, since she wasn't used to it.

I had never expected to have privacy while dating a celebrity, so it wasn't a huge deal for me to not have it with Lacey. Then again, the media was being harsher on her than on me. I wanted to keep her safe and comfortable, so we decided to stay away from each other for a few days while we figured out what to do next.

My parents' opinion was that I should never talk to Lacey again. Although they'd liked her well enough when they'd met, they hated the bad publicity she was creating for me. They thought it reflected negatively on them. I wasn't about to give her up, so I'd promised I'd do my best to keep our relationship quiet for the moment. That was what we'd been planning to do anyway, so I didn't mind.

"What have you been up to?" I asked her over the phone, sitting in bed as usual as Jason sat in the armchair a few feet away.

"Just researching job opportunities and putting in applications." She sounded tired, and maybe frustrated. "No bites so far."

"You'll find something soon."

"I don't know," she said. "The agency isn't going to give me a reference because of the way I left."

"I'll give you a reference," I said. "Excellent worker, A+ communication skills, absolutely amazing in bed…"

Footsteps creaked from Jason's direction. Apparently he was going to find something to do somewhere else.

"Thanks," Lacey said. "I'm sure that'll be helpful."

"Seriously," I said. "You're amazing at what you do."

"In bed?"

"And outside it." I smiled. "You never took any of my shit, and that's rare."

"I know. That's why you like me."

I snorted. "I like you *despite* that." I knew I was lying.

"Anyway, when do you think we'll be able to meet up again?" she asked, her voice suddenly softer.

"That's up to you," I said. "ASAP, ideally, but I don't really know how we're going to avoid reporters. I really thought renting the whole restaurant for ourselves would do it, but I guess they're watching my place." I didn't know if they were camping out there, or what. Didn't these people have lives?

"Maybe you should come to mine," Lacey said.

My breath caught in my throat. I hadn't expected her to invite me over, at least not yet. She lived with her parents, after all. Was I ready to meet them? Was I even ready to visit her place if they weren't around? That would make this whole thing real. It'd be impossible to forget I was dating someone non-famous.

I quickly imagined what her place might look like. Tiny, for sure. Cramped, like one of the regular people's houses I saw on TV. Would it be dark and grimy, too? Was it just her and her parents, or did they share it with anyone else?

The whole idea was intimidating, but it did seem safer than having her over here again. If I wanted to be with her – and I did – then this was going to happen eventually.

"Are you sure?" I asked, almost hoping she'd say no.

"Yes," she said after a brief hesitation. "Come over tonight. I'll make dinner."

"Oh, forget it, then."

She shrieked with indignation. "You've never even had my cooking!"

"You've told me enough about it." I cackled. "I'm not ready to sink to that level."

"You better be joking." She sounded threatening.

"Yeah, I am."

I hadn't been joking, but I'd try her food.

If it was that bad, I'd find a way to sneak it to Jason.

*

We pulled up in her driveway at six-thirty that night. It didn't seem like we'd been followed, especially since I'd had Jason take a winding route with a lot of extra twists and turns. The last thing I needed was for the paparazzi to find out where Lacey lived.

The house was smaller than I'd expected, if that was even possible. It looked exactly the same as every house on the block, at least from the outside – one story tall, with a white-trim exterior and a postage-stamp lawn.

Jason helped me out of the car, and with my crutches, I got to the front door. I'd worn a floppy hat and dark sunglasses just in case, and Lacey burst into laughter when she saw me. "Hey there, Carmen Sandiego."

"Shush and get inside."

The place looked a bit better on the inside. Although the hallway was narrow and the ceiling was low, the windows let in natural light and the tile floors were spotless. I tried not to cringe as I looked at the decades-old furniture.

Then my attention was distracted from

everything else when I noticed a near-clone of Lacey.

"You must be Zana," the woman said. "I'm Juliet Howard. It's nice to meet you." Without further notice, she pulled me into a hug.

I stumbled, caught off-balance with the way I'd been leaning on my crutches, and she let me go. I took a breath as I looked at her more closely. She and Lacey really were each other's doubles, although it was clear that Juliet was quite a bit older.

I hadn't quite been ready to see her here, even though I'd known meeting might be possible. I hadn't met Tia's parents in the six months we'd been together, and I'd figured that was normal. Now Lacey had me meeting her mom before we were even official.

Hopefully this was a good sign – a sign that she'd eventually agree to become my official girlfriend.

"It's lovely to meet you," I said. "This is my new care worker, Jason."

We headed inside, and the smell of fresh herbs greeted me in the kitchen. "What is that?" I asked.

"I made meatloaf," Lacey said shyly. "It's nothing gourmet or anything, but…"

"What other talents have you been hiding from me?" I peeked into the oven, where the meatloaf was sizzling away. "If that tastes as good as it smells, I should've hired you as my personal chef." I realized I was talking about her as an employee again, and hastily corrected myself. "But now that we're dating, you can share mine. Unless you want to cook, in which case you're welcome to."

She put her hand on my shoulder. "Let's hope you like it."

The meal went by fast. Juliet was more talkative than Lacey, and her favorite topic was her daughter. By the end of dinner, I felt like I'd gotten a whole new perspective on her.

"I can't believe you never mentioned you skipped third grade," I told her. "You were, like, some kind of baby genius or something."

"It doesn't come up often." Her cheeks were pink. "I'm going to clean up. You go in the living room and find something to watch on TV."

"I'll clean up," Juliet interjected.

"I would offer to help, but it might be a bit hard." I gestured at my bad arm. "I'll have to give you a hand next time."

Juliet smiled at me. "That means you're planning to visit again. Sounds good to me."

Lacey, Jason, and I headed into the living room, and she handed me the remote. I tossed it aside. "I have to say, watching TV isn't actually what I want to do right now."

"Oh?" she asked flirtatiously.

"Um…" Jason said. "I'm just going to… see if your mom needs help. Yeah. I'll be in the kitchen, if you need me. Or if you decide to go upstairs, that's where you can find me… later."

We both giggled as he made his exit. Then she was in my arms, kissing me hard and returning all the passion that'd been building up inside me for the past few days. It felt like forever since I'd seen her, felt her, and I'd almost forgotten how incredible it was to be with her.

"So… upstairs?" she asked breathlessly when we pulled apart.

"As long as there are no reporters up there, that sounds *great* to me."

Twenty-Four – Lacey

The next two weeks were like a dream.
Suddenly I was at Zana's place every day again,
or she was at mine. We'd decided the paparazzi
would have enough of our relationship
eventually, so we were ignoring them and
hoping they'd go away. So far, they were still
writing about us all the time, always looking for
new ways to smear my name, but the fuss had
slowed down to some extent.

Instead of me working for Zana, we just hung
out and enjoyed each other's company – in more
ways than one. She always had Jason or Karen
around to take care of anything she couldn't
handle physically, so I never had to lift a finger.

That wasn't to say everything was perfect. She
was still selfish – to the point that I still
wondered if I was crazy for getting involved
with her. She could be short with the care
workers, even if she was nothing but kind to me.

But more and more, I was seeing a side of her
she didn't show too often. It wasn't the perfect
princess image she put on for the public, or the
prickly pear she'd been when we first met. It
was just her – the true, genuine her.

Around five weeks after her accident, we lay in
bed through most of the morning. I was reading
on my Kindle while she browsed Twitter on her

tablet. Occasionally, she showed me a funny image or a cat video. Otherwise, we were silent.

After lunch, she called Jason. "Could you get me some of the textbooks that are in my closet? They should be on the top shelf."

"I'll do it." I stood up. After being in bed for so long, my limbs needed a stretch. "Which textbooks do you want?"

"Whatever's in there. I don't really care."

I frowned, confused, but I assumed she'd explain herself after. I went into her closet, which was practically the size of my room, and dug around. It only took me a minute to find a giant stack of books. Psychology, philosophy, English, drama. They would've been more obvious, but they'd been hidden by her even larger amount of clothes.

"Here you go," I said, depositing a few of the books on her left side. "Are you thinking of going back to school, or something?"

"Back?" She lifted a textbook onto her lap and flicked the cover open. "I'm in school."

My stomach turned over. "You… are?"

"I'm enrolled, yes." She twisted her body so she could look at me. "I can't look down at the pages. I'm going to have to figure something out."

"But…" My mind was short-circuiting. "Your classes. Your lessons. Your notes."

"What about them?"

Suddenly I felt like her home care worker again. This would've been a fireable offense, if I hadn't already been fired. "Nothing about this was in your file, and you didn't say anything. They'll have to understand you were in an accident, though, won't they? You can easily get a doctor's note. Or were you studying at night after I left?"

"What are you talking about?"

Her casual attitude had me mystified. Was I freaking out for no reason? She must've not studied for five weeks – more, considering her time in the hospital before I started here. Maybe she could still catch up.

Rubbing my temples, I shook my head. "So you're feeling that much better? You can focus on studying now, and you couldn't before?"

"Of course I could focus before. I just didn't feel like it."

I let my hands fall as I stared at her. Her expression was open and guileless. She really saw nothing wrong with what she was saying.

"You're in college, and you didn't… feel like… studying?" I asked.

"It's not like I went to classes before. I haven't been studying any less than I usually do, anyway." She laughed – as if it was funny.

My blood boiled. I thought I'd gotten over her

spoiled, lazy, entitled attitude. I thought things had changed between us – that dating had made everything better. In the space of a single minute, she'd just sent our relationship straight back to square one.

"You know people would give their left arm to have the opportunity you have, don't you?"

She laughed again, nervously this time. "I gave my right arm." She raised her cast. "Right leg and neck, too."

"I'll be back in a minute," I said, quietly seething. "I need to – I just – yeah."

I ran out to the kitchen, where I opened the freezer door and stuck my head inside, hoping it would cool me off. It didn't.

Enrolling in college just to skip classes and fail out was on a whole other level. I couldn't imagine how someone could waste their money like that, squander their privilege. And then there was Zana, doing it in front of me, laughing about it? She made me sick.

Standing straight, I forced myself to take a breath. Zana wasn't me. She'd never lacked for money in her life. Of course she didn't appreciate its value.

Still, I couldn't understand how she could be so ungrateful! When I'd been in college, there was no way I'd ever go two weeks without mentioning it. I'd talked about it every day, telling everyone who would listen about the courses I was taking and all the cool things I was learning. I wouldn't shut up about how excited I was to become a nurse.

Then Grandma had died, and all the money I'd saved for my next semester had gone to her funeral expenses. Compare that to Zana, a stupid brat who had everything I'd ever wanted and didn't appreciate any of it.

I let my hands close into fists, my fingernails digging into my palms. I needed to calm down. I'd had a rough deal, but Zana wasn't me. What we had was more important than her riches. I needed to be happy for her, not jealous.

If I was going to date her, I couldn't think of her as a brat. She'd had a hard time in different ways than I had.

And I did want to keep dating her. I did.

Forcing a smile onto my face, I headed back into her bedroom. "So, tell me more about your classes," I said. "What college is it? What's your major?"

Looking worried, she told me she was taking a liberal arts degree at UCLA.

I sat next to her and propped a book up in her lap, setting it against a couple of other books so it wouldn't fall. "You should be able to look through your books if we rig them up like this."

Now that I knew she was in school, I was damn well going to make sure she took it seriously.

TWENTY-FIVE – ZANA

I set my phone aside and reached for my philosophy textbook. A minute into looking at it, and my eyes were already glazing over. The ancient words of Aristotle and Socrates just couldn't keep my attention the way my Twitter feed could. Even when people trashed Lacey, I felt compelled to read every word.

The book fell down in my lap, and I closed my eyes with a sigh. Was there even a point to trying to study? The semester was more than halfway over, and I hadn't even looked at a course outline until the other day. I was going to fail out of all my courses no matter what I did. It'd be smarter to forget about this semester and try again next term.

I just felt like doing *something.* Being with Lacey made me want to be a better person. She was so smart, so driven. She'd worked so hard when she was working for me, and even now, she spent all her time job-searching when she wasn't over here. Whenever she talked about her time in nursing school, she got this wistful look in her eye.

I was never going to be like that, but I could at least try to not be completely useless. I'd always gotten good marks in school when I bothered to put in the effort – which wasn't often. After having a private teacher all my life, I'd found college strange and confusing, and I'd tried even less.

I'd do better now that I had Lacey to inspire me. In the meantime, I planned to get her back into nursing school. I just had to find a way to do it without injuring her pride. There was no way she'd accept a huge cash gift, at least not this early in our relationship.

I'd see how things went once I was out of these damn casts. Everything would be different once we could spend more time outside my place. That day was coming up soon. On my last doctor's appointment, they said I was healing well and there was no reason I couldn't be walking again in a little over two weeks.

I'd need a lot of physiotherapy and rehabilitative work, of course, but being out of the casts was a major first step. I couldn't wait to stretch my atrophying limbs and wash them in the shower, not to mention taking a dip in my indoor pool. Oh, and I was going to scratch the *fuck* out of that spot that'd been itching for a month.

Lacey sat down on the bed next to me and peered over the top of my book. "*Ancient Philosophy?* Which concepts are you studying?"

"I don't even know," I sighed. "It's so boring. I can't make myself give a shit."

Her lips pursed. "You have to focus, babe. You signed up for this course for a reason."

"Sure, because a philosophy course is required for my degree."

"There must be more to it than that."

"Nope, nothing." I pushed the book aside. "Come here and kiss me."

"No kisses until you tell me..." She flipped through the book again. "What the allegory of the cave is about."

"I have no fucking idea!" I leaned forward, pulling her toward me with my good arm. "No studying. Just make-outs."

"It's not exactly a turn-on when you act like a child who has to be coaxed into studying." She let out a sigh. "I want you to care about your schoolwork. Not everyone has the privilege of getting to go to school."

"To go to school." I said the last few words along with her – she gave me the same speech so often that I knew it by heart.

"Oh, you're mocking me now?"

She looked furious, and I knew I shouldn't have used that tone. "It's too late for me to pass this semester, okay?" I said more gently. "It's a write-off. I just need to start over next semester."

"You could pass if you tried. You just don't want to."

"Do you really think I could learn a whole semester's worth of five courses in the next four weeks?" I shook my head. "Exams are in a month, Lace. I'm not some kind of genius."

"Then why were you studying?" She gestured at the book that was still beside me. "You must've thought you had a chance."

"If anything, I thought studying now would help me next semester, but…" I sighed. "It's just so goddamn boring."

She made a face, and I knew she was disapproving again. In her world, saying school was boring was damn near sacrilegious.

I did understand the value of education, I really did, but it wasn't like I'd ever struggle to pay for it. If UCLA kicked me out for failing this semester – which wasn't likely, seeing as I'd failed all my other courses so far – I'd just bring my business to another college.

"If it's that boring, maybe you're in the wrong program," she said curtly. "Why did you choose liberal arts?"

"I dunno. Seemed easy."

She glared at me. "What are you planning to do with your degree afterwards?"

"Same as I'm doing now, probably." If I even managed to get the degree, which was also unlikely.

"You're really planning to just lie around and live off your parents for your whole life?" she asked. "You don't have any other ambitions? You don't even want to help people?"

She was getting on my nerves a little now. "It's *my* life," I snapped. "If I want to live a life of leisure, I'm allowed to. And considering how my parents screwed me over since birth, they owe it to me to support me."

"What about independence?" she asked. "Don't you have any pride?"

My eyebrows shot up. "You just went too far."

She got up, cutting our conversation short, and I sat back in bed, willing my pounding heart to calm down.

Was this our first fight? If so, we hadn't resolved it well. I'd gotten heated, she'd gotten heated, and in the end, I'd freaked out because…

She was right.

TWENTY-SIX – LACEY

I balanced my laptop on my thighs, my feet on the living-room coffee table. My eyes were going numb from staring at the screen all morning, and I still hadn't gotten a single response to a job application.

"Lacey, would you mind picking up a few groceries later on today?" Mom asked, appearing in the doorway. Taking me in, she frowned. "Wait, why do you look so miserable?"

Heaving a sigh, I set the laptop aside. "I've been job-hunting for almost three weeks, and no one is interested in what I have to offer. This is soul-sucking."

"Oh, sweetie, someone will give you a chance. They're bound to."

"If they haven't yet, when's it going to happen?" I couldn't even blame the employers. I wouldn't have hired someone who was known to have slept with a client, even if the relationship had only started after I'd already been let go. "And I can't take much more of this abuse online. People hate me, and they don't even know me."

An especially hateful tweet had referred to me with words I wished I could erase from my brain. I had to stop looking at what people said online, but somehow I kept going back for more, as if I was punishing myself for finally being happy.

"Why don't you go over to Zana's place, then?" Mom asked. "Relax and try to enjoy the time off. It may seem like a crazy idea now, but once you're working again, you'll wonder why you didn't make the best of your free time."

"I can't." I put my chin into my hands. "I have to find a job, Mom. What if we can't even make rent this month and it's all because of me?"

It'd crossed my mind to ask Zana for help. The money would've been nothing to her, less than a drop in the bucket. But asking for a hand-out went against everything I'd ever held dear. Even if I'd done it, my parents wouldn't have accepted the money.

"Maybe I can get an advance on my next paycheck," Mom said.

Fuck… that was just as bad. I didn't want to put her out like that. It'd make her look bad to her boss, and she'd probably have to pay crazy amounts of interest on the loan. But there was no way I'd go to Zana, either.

There was only one solution – I had to find a job.

"We'll talk about this later," I said. "Write out the grocery list, and I'll pick everything up when I have a chance. You go enjoy your day off."

With a worried look, she left.

I picked the laptop up again and checked my

email hopefully. Maybe a nice, open-minded employer had written me in the last three minutes. Nope, nothing there – but a Tia fan had somehow found my personal address and wanted me to know I was a giant bitch.

Unable to think about refreshing the job search page again, I grabbed my phone for a quick break. A new message from Zana popped up, and I smiled as I opened it. Even though there'd been some tension between us for the last couple days because of her attitude toward school, hearing from her always made me happy.

Just got my casts off! she'd texted. *Guess who has TWO working hands and can't wait to put them all over you?!*

My jaw dropped. She'd gotten them off today? It'd been six weeks since her accident already? I'd just seen her yesterday, and she hadn't mentioned a thing about going back to the doctor!

Um, what?!? I wrote back. *OMG! Are you home? I'm coming over!*

Come this afternoon. They're still cutting this thing off my neck!

*

At two o'clock on the dot, I arrived on Zana's doorstep with a plate of just-baked brownies and a homemade card reading *About Damn Time*

You Got Well!

I fidgeted as I waited for her to come and open the door. Everything was going to be different now that she was healed. We could be alone without constantly having Jason or Karen around, for one thing. And she'd be able to go anywhere, do anything she wanted.

It'd take some time for her to go through physio, of course, but soon she'd be completely back to normal. And I'd never known her normal. From what I'd gathered, she was constantly on the move, active both physically and socially. She liked to go out, always checking out a trendy new place and spending piles of money.

Would the normal her even want anything to do with me?

She opened the door, and I immediately screeched. Her neck brace was off, and she grinned as she turned her head from one side to the other.

"Oh my God, this is amazing!" I wrapped her in a hug, and she hugged me back – with both arms! "I never thought I'd see the day."

"Did you really think I'd be in those casts until I died?"

"It kind of felt like it." I came further inside and slipped off my shoes, then touched her right arm in wonder again. "How was it getting them off? Did it hurt? How do they feel now?"

"One question at a time," she said, leading me

toward the staircase. "Actually, ask me later. There's something I want to do first."

"Oh?" A spark leapt through me, sending heat through my core. "What might that be?"

Pausing to turn back to look at me, she grinned. "I told you, I want to put both these hands all over you."

"And we have to go upstairs for that?"

Her smile got even wider as she stepped close to me and grabbed my ass. "We can start right here."

TWENTY-SEVEN – ZANA

I lay in bed next to Lacey, scrolling through Twitter on my phone. She was still sleeping, and I resisted the urge to take a picture to tease her with later. She looked too damn adorable right now.

I was so happy that I could use both hands to hold my phone again. I'd never take my healthy, working body for granted again. It was funny how I used to obsess over gaining an extra inch on my waist. I'd spent so much time agonizing about whether or not I should get a boob job. Now I was just grateful that my limbs worked and I wasn't in pain.

I was grateful for Lacey's presence, too. I barely remembered who I'd been before her, and I didn't even want to think about not having her in my life. It was crazy, considering I'd only known her for two months and been dating for one. And I'd thought so little of her at first – now I wondered how I'd gotten by without her.

We'd gotten into a nice routine lately. She'd come over and send out resumes while I studied for my college exams. She used to stay home to focus better, but now we'd gotten the hang of working silently together. I was pretty sure I was still going to fail everything, but she liked to see me study, so I did it anyway. I had to admit,

I focused better when she was around.

A message arrived, and I stopped scrolling to click on it. The sender was Kaidee. Now, that was a name I hadn't thought about in a while. It was funny – the group of us had hung out at least two or three times a week before my accident. I hadn't heard from her or Gemini or Brittney while I'd been recovering, not since I'd gotten out of the hospital.

When I'd briefly thought about them, I'd figured Tia was keeping them in the break-up. They'd been my friends first, but Tia had really bonded with them. She always wanted to meet up with them rather than spending time with me alone.

Hey girl! the message read. *How you feeling? Back on your feet yet? We're all going skydiving soon!! xoxoxox*

I frowned as I read it again. No apologies for not being in touch for so long… no acknowledgment of all the pain I'd been in… She just expected me to go skydiving with them as if nothing had ever happened.

Still, she'd reached out. That meant she was thinking of me. This experience had taught me I needed some new friends… but for now, these girls were all I had.

Besides, skydiving did sound amazing. What better way to celebrate being able to walk again?

Instead of texting back, I dialed her number. "Morning!" I exclaimed. "How've you been?"

"Great!" Kaidee said. "Oh my gosh, you've missed so much stuff going on. I have a ton of gossip to catch you up on! Did you know Michael Atkinson followed Gemini on Instagram?"

Really? That was what she wanted to talk about – that some D-list actor had followed our friend on social media? I'd barely gotten off bed rest, and she didn't have a single question to ask about my recovery?

"That's great," I said tightly.

She waited for me to say more. When I didn't, she kept talking away with no change in her frantic energy. "Wouldn't they make the cutest couple? I can just picture her going to the Oscars with him! I mean, he'd look better with me, of course, but I already have plans to go... with..."

She was pausing for dramatic effect, but I wasn't going to take the bait. Not today. "So, you mentioned skydiving?" I asked, looking at Lacey as she shifted in bed – my conversation had almost woken her up. I got up and went into the hall as I continued. "I just got my casts off the other day. Where would you be going, and when?"

"Oh, you want to go! Perfect!" She seemed like she was trying to sound enthusiastic – I assumed because she still wanted to talk about her Oscars date. "It's this weekend. We were thinking Hawaii."

"Ugh, I've been to Hawaii so many times." The

skydiving was amazing there, but it was like been there, done that.

"How about Alaska, then?"

"Sure, that sounds good." I leaned against the doorframe, smiling at how adorable Lacey looked. "I'm going to bring someone, if that's all right."

She hesitated. "Of course!" she said, a little too brightly.

We hung up, and I went back over to Lacey. I hated to wake her up, but I hoped she'd wake on her own. The bed moving as I sat down did the trick. "Morning, beautiful," I said, and kissed her on the cheek. "Do you have a ski jacket? Warm clothes?"

"Huh?" She blinked up at me.

"We're going skydiving in Alaska this weekend."

She sat up, her sleepiness vanishing. "*What?*"

"You want to come, don't you? I'll pay your way, obviously." I rubbed her shoulder. "You can meet a few of my friends. They'll like you." Hopefully, anyway. There might be some awkwardness at me replacing Tia so fast, but that was Tia's own fault.

Actually, it might be awkward for those girls to hang out with someone who wasn't famous at all and had zero Instagram followers. And for Lacey to be surrounded by, well, people like me.

I could just imagine her yelling at them for disrespecting the maids or under-tipping the wait staff.

But if that happened, I'd be on her side. Maybe she'd be a good influence on my friends – Lord knew they needed it. And if they were snobby for one second or talked any shit about Lacey, I'd be there to defend her.

"I don't know if I'm into skydiving," she said slowly.

The expression on her face perplexed me. Was that… was she… *scared?*

I laughed out loud, amazed by my own realization. Lacey Howard, the queen of stoicism, the woman who'd walk into a celebrity's mansion and treat her like a disobedient child, was terrified of something as simple as skydiving.

"Don't be such a wimp," I said, massaging her neck. "It's going to be fun."

"It's literally jumping out of a plane!"

"Like I said," I laughed. "Fun."

TWENTY-EIGHT – LACEY

With the beginning of the month rapidly approaching, my job search was still on. There was no way I'd earn a paycheck by the time rent was due, but at least I'd actually landed an interview. The position was similar to what I'd been doing with Zana up until my abrupt dismissal. The pay was actually a little better, and the possible locations were spread throughout the city.

"You're going to do great," Mom said in the morning, straightening my collar. "I'd like to press this shirt one more time, but – "

"I have to go!" I darted out of her grasp. "I already ironed the shirt. It'll be fine."

"It just has that one tiny wrinkle."

"If they want to hire me, one wrinkle isn't going to stop them." And if they didn't want to hire me, well, they wouldn't.

I was as prepared as I was going to be. I'd stayed up late practicing interview answers in front of the mirror. I'd researched the company until I could spout their FAQ page off by heart. I'd tied my hair into a tight bun and, of course, I'd worn a freshly-ironed blouse.

I drove to the interview location, nervous but optimistic. Zana had been so excited when I told her about the interview, and I didn't want to let her down. I knew she was perplexed by my need to work – if it'd been up to her, she would've given me a few thousand in cash and taken a month off job-hunting.

Even though she didn't understand, she still cheered me on with a passion. She asked questions about the positions I was applying to and helped me think about how the job I took now would affect my long-term career.

I stepped out of the car and pasted a smile on my face. I easily found the interview room, and my smile grew more genuine as I shook the kind-looking older woman's hand. If there was anyone in the world unaffected by social media, I was pretty sure it was her.

"Tell me about your last position," Wendy said, getting immediately to the topic I'd feared. "What did you do there?"

"It was similar to this one." I gave a brief description of the tasks I'd done for Zana every day – not including fighting my attraction or going to the Grammys with her.

"And why did you leave?"

I winced. Wasn't it illegal to ask that, or something? "I thought it was time to move on," I said carefully. "I wanted to take on some new challenges."

"Interesting," Wendy said, looking again at my resume. "Well, you certainly seem qualified. I have other applicants to interview, but I can say now that you're a very promising candidate. I don't see any reason we wouldn't offer you the job – unless there's anything we don't know about."

Was this a test? Was I supposed to *volunteer* the information about Zana? I tried to smile, fighting down the sick feeling in my stomach. What was better, to tell her I'd been fired and potentially not get the job, or to keep it to myself and risk getting found out later?

"I don't think there's anything you're missing," I finally said. "I'll be looking forward to hearing your decision."

"Great. It was very nice to meet you." Wendy stood up and extended her hand.

I shook it... but the sick feeling hadn't gone away, and I suspected it wouldn't until I told the truth.

"There is one thing you should know," I said quietly. "I... was actually let go from my last job. I gave the appearance of being romantically involved with my patient, even though nothing actually happened until I wasn't employed there anymore. I don't want to start off our professional relationship by being dishonest with you. There've been a lot of rude things written about me online, so if you happen to Google me, all of this will come up."

Her eyes widened almost imperceptibly. "Thank you for your candor. You'll be hearing from us shortly… one way or the other."

*

"Why would you tell her the truth?" Zana demanded when I arrived at her place. "You could've lost the job because of that."

"Or I could've gotten it," I said. "Besides, now I can sleep easily knowing I did the right thing."

She shook her head. "You're impossible."

"Better for her to hear it from me now than to Google me and wonder why I kept it from her."

"I guess." She made a face. "Anyway, we're going skydiving tomorrow! Are you ready?"

"No."

I wasn't too keen on any part of the skydiving thing, from the plane we'd be taking to Alaska, to the one we'd be jumping out of. I had no particular urge to meet her friends, either. They'd totally ignored her for six weeks, and now they were going to act like nothing had even happened? I'd kind of hoped she'd just stop talking to them entirely, but I wasn't going to tell her that.

I didn't like the fact that she was paying for me, either. Between the flight and the activity, it was going to be more expensive than I wanted to think about. That was her choice, though. And it wasn't like she was just handing me money.

She'd be there doing it with me.

"You'll try to have fun, though, won't you?" she asked, a slight whine to her voice. "I don't want to drag you there and have you hate every minute of it."

"Yeah, yeah." I'd try to enjoy it for her sake. She was enthusiastic about it, and it was nice to see her excited about something. She'd been through so much lately – she deserved to have a good time.

And who knew? Maybe I'd have a secret passion for feeling like I was about to die.

Twenty-Nine – Zana

LAX bustled with activity. There were so many people, it was hard to even know where to go. I pushed up my sunglasses, wishing I could take them off but not wanting to be recognized. A hand waved in my direction, and I squinted, unsure if it was a fan or a friend.

Realizing it was Kaidee, I grabbed Lacey's hand and hurried in her direction – then stopped short.

Gemini was also there, and so was Brittney… and Tia.

Lacey whipped her head toward me, clearly recognizing Tia. The look on her face said, *You didn't tell me she was going to be here.*

I gave her a tiny, apologetic shrug, hoping she understood that meant I hadn't known either.

"He-e-ey," I said awkwardly. "Guys, this is Lacey. She's coming with us this weekend. Lacey, this is Kaidee and Gemini and Brittney and Tia."

"Right," Lacey said, glaring daggers at Tia. "We've met before… briefly."

"This isn't weird, is it?" Kaidee asked. "I mean, you two broke up, but you're still friends." She gestured at me and Tia.

I snorted. Who'd told her that? I'd been under the impression that Tia and I were never going to talk again, and I'd kind of liked it that way.

It was weird just seeing her again, never mind spending a whole weekend trip with her. I could see why I'd been drawn to her – her porcelain features and hourglass figure would've attracted anyone. But now there was an ugliness to her as well, and I knew I was looking at what lay below the surface.

I'd seen the real her now, and it wasn't the sickly-sweet woman she'd pretended to be during our relationship. I cringed as I thought back to the times she'd told me she loved me or called me "baby." It'd all been an act, and I'd fallen for it hook, line, and sinker.

Yeah, there was nothing I wanted less than to spend the weekend with Tia. Did I have a choice, though? I'd already bought the tickets and harassed Lacey into coming. The money didn't matter, but I wasn't sure if I'd be able to convince her a second time. Besides, I'd already gotten pumped to jump out of that plane. I'd been craving the adrenaline rush for the past few days.

"No," I said tightly. "It's not weird."

I kept my distance from Tia as we went through the check-in line and security. I held Lacey's hand, whispering apologies to her every two minutes. I hoped she understood how terrible I felt for bringing her into this situation, especially when she hadn't wanted to come in the first place.

Once we were in the departures lounge, we sat down and chatted a bit. Gemini was sympathetic to the ordeal I'd been through, even if Kaidee still didn't seem to care. Surprisingly, Brittney was friendly to Lacey, asking her some getting-to-know-you questions. "Where are you from? What do you do?"

"I'm a care worker," she said. "I used to be Zana's care worker."

They must've known that already – I was sure every one of them had tracked down every article about us that'd ever been posted. Even so, Gemini wrinkled her nose ever so slightly, and Tia didn't bother to hide her look of disgust.

"Are you working now?" Brittney asked.

"No, I'm looking for a new job at the moment."

I knew this was a touchy issue for Lacey, and yet she was completely calm and collected. A swell of pride and affection went through me. I never should've doubted she could hold her own with these girls, no matter how catty and judgmental they might get.

The four of them looked at each other, and I could've sworn Tia mouthed an "ew." I bristled, wanting to scream at her and tell her not to disrespect Lacey like that. But Lacey was looking into the distance – she must not have seen. The only thing yelling would do was cause a scene.

By the time we got to Alaska, Tia had made a few openly snide comments. Even though Lacey and I had been in a different row, we'd overheard everything the others had said, and her optimistic smile had been replaced by a dull look.

I squeezed her knee as we exited the plane. As soon as I could, I was going to catch Tia alone and give her a talking-to.

That moment came when we got to our hotel. Lacey and the others went ahead to put our bags in the suite, and I caught Tia by the arm and dragged her further down the hall.

"Wow," she said, eyeing me flirtatiously. "I knew you'd be desperate to get me back, but I didn't think you'd start trying this fast."

I stared at her. "What? You do realize I'm here with another girl, right?"

"And you're dragging me into the hall for a make-out session. Classy. I guess you really missed me."

"I didn't, actually. I'm here with Lacey."

"Can we stop with the Lacey thing?" She rolled her eyes. "It's gone on long enough. It's getting ridiculous."

"Excuse me?"

"She's a *care worker*. You're not going to seriously date her."

"I already started." Even though we hadn't officially put a label on our relationship – something I planned to do as soon as possible. "You broke up with me, so don't act like I'm doing something wrong."

"I asked you for a break," she snapped.

"No, you didn't. You dumped me! You had the world's worst reason, too. I was a downer because I was injured?"

Another eye roll, bigger this time. "Of course you were, and clearly you still are. It should've been obvious that once you were better, we'd be getting back together."

I huffed out a laugh. "Excuse me? So what, I was supposed to wait around at home while you ran around screwing whoever you wanted, and then once I was healed we'd pick things back up like nothing ever happened?"

"It sounds so shady when you put it that way."

"Because it is shady!" My anger was rising. Had my friends set up this whole weekend to get us back together? "You were planning to use me, Tia. If you wanted to sleep with other people so bad, why would you come back to me at all?"

"Because I *love* you," she said.

"No, you don't." I doubted she knew what the word meant.

Something flashed across her face. "Of course I do. We had six great months together. Doesn't that matter to you?"

"Stop fucking lying."

"Fine!" She let the mask drop, and the expression that'd been on her face a minute before came back. Hostility, or maybe spite. "I'll tell you the truth. Your mom reached out to me, all right? She said she wants this whole thing with Lacey to go away, and that she can't get through to you about it."

My stomach dropped. Could she be making this up? I wanted to think she was – but I was pretty sure this was finally the truth.

"She went to you?" I whispered.

My mother had asked me several times to cut things off with Lacey. My dad had tried, too. Each had offered various incentives and bribes. I hadn't listened. I'd told them things would blow over eventually, and then I'd hung up on them. I hadn't cheated on Tia, after all. I hadn't done *anything* wrong.

But they'd gone to Tia? That was hitting below the belt. I'd cared about this girl, even if I hadn't felt as strongly as I did for Lacey. She'd hurt me, and my parents were still trying to make her a pawn in their game?

"She offered me a mill." I would've thought Tia would look ashamed. Instead, she appeared to be excited. "Another year of dating, and then we were going to renegotiate for the next year. I wasn't really supposed to tell you, but I don't think it's a big deal. You can talk to her and make your own deal. She'll probably give you even more than me. Your parents are made of money."

My throat was dry. "Was this their doing in the first place? Were they paying you all along?"

"No, no, no," she said soothingly. "Of course not. The public just happened to love us together, and your parents want things to be the way they used to be. What do you say, Zana?" Her arm snaked around my waist. "Things could be just like before, except we'd be even richer."

"I don't want to be paid to date you," I hissed, stepping away. "I want to be with the woman I actually care about, who cares about me."

"We were good together," she said. "Remember?"

I remembered, all right. I remembered posing for pictures with our arms around each other, our smiles dropping once the camera flash went off. Making up lovey-dovey stories to tweet out that had nothing to do with what'd actually happened. Giving interviews about how she was the best thing to ever happen to me, and then sitting together in silence because we had nothing to say to each other.

Now that I looked back on it, even if I hadn't been paid, the whole relationship felt like a lie. And I might've never realized it if I hadn't found something actually real with Lacey.

"I'm going to take a pass," I said. "Thanks, but no thanks."

"Have it your way," she said bitterly. "But when your relationship with that home care worker falls apart, you'll regret not taking this offer."

THIRTY – LACEY

The morning was bright and clear, and everything would've been great if Zana hadn't been acting all weird since last night. She'd been quiet since we got to the hotel, and I had to suspect that had something to do with her ex's presence.

I believed her when she said she hadn't known Tia would be coming. I just wasn't sure if she cared as little as she claimed. Tia was beautiful and famous, an equal match for Zana. Me, on the other hand? I definitely wasn't.

I clung to her hand as we stood in line at the skydiving facility. Funny how I'd been hesitant to start anything up with her, and now I was terrified of it ending. I wasn't ready for this to be over. And it had nothing to do with being whisked away to exotic destinations to take part in extreme sports. I didn't want to stop spending time with Zana, no matter where we were or what we were doing.

"Get your ID out," she said as we approached the front of the line. "They're going to have to check it."

Reluctantly, I dropped her hand and did as she said. I was going to have to take a class to learn how to skydive, which somehow made me feel better and worse about the whole thing. It was good that it wasn't as simple as jumping out of a plane, but on the other hand, a more complicated process meant there was more potential for me to mess up – and die.

"You're not going to die," Zana whispered in my ear, patting me on the butt as she pointed me toward the lesson room. "Listen hard, and I'll see you afterwards."

The rest of them seemed to have been skydiving since birth, so they didn't have to take the class. I felt bad for holding them up… and queasy at the thought of Zana with Tia without me. Would they click during the next hour and end up getting back together? A year from now, would they laugh over the story of the time Zana had brought her care worker as her date for a weekend away?

If that was going to happen, there was nothing I could do. I gave her a kiss on the cheek and went into the room with the other newbies. Thankfully, the instructor was funny, and the lesson went by fast. My nerves eased when he said all of us would be tandem jumping with an instructor. I still had a feeling I might die, but now the chances were a little lower.

Zana found me as soon as I left the room. "You're still here?" I asked. "I thought all of you might've jumped already."

"Of course not, silly. I'm jumping with you. The others have gone ahead."

I frowned. "The guy said I had to go with a

licensed instructor."

"Yeah, me." She laughed at my look of confusion – maybe her first genuine laugh since last night. "I logged so many hours of skydiving a few years back, I figured I might as well get certified."

"Oh."

It was nice that she'd chosen to go with me rather than her other friends. That made me feel a little more secure. But… did I really trust her to keep me safe? I'd seen how seriously she took studying for her college courses – or didn't take it, rather. But clearly she was passionate about skydiving, and she'd gotten through a number of jumps alive.

"I had to log five hundred jumps to get my certification," she said. "Three hours of freefall."

"Jesus." Shock took over my dubiousness. "That's a lot of fucking jumping."

"It's addictive." She grinned. "You'll find out."

*

Twenty minutes later, we stood in the middle of a tiny plane, looking down at the closed hatch that we'd soon be jumping out of. I hadn't mentioned it to her, but yesterday had been my first time in any kind of plane, and that'd been terrifying enough. Now I was supposed to jump out of one?

She looked at my pale face. "It's okay," she said. "It's going to be fun."

I doubted that. I already felt like I was about to puke. As long as I could walk out of this day alive, I'd be happy. It'd just figure if I broke all the bones in my body so soon after helping her recover. Seriously, what was she thinking, starting up with the extreme sports again so soon?

"Get in your harness." She held it out for me, and I vaguely remembered the class instructor showing us how to step inside.

Once I was in, she opened the hatch and strapped my back to her front. Oh, shit... this'd just gotten a whole lot realer.

I made bargains in my mind. As long as I made it out alive, I wouldn't complain about breaking a bone or two. I'd shut up about money and not having a job. I wouldn't even care if Zana broke up with me.

Actually, that was going too far. I'd still care, very much, if she broke up with me.

My heart pounded as I looked out at the snow-covered mountains below. I blinked, and when they were still there, a wave of disbelief hit me. I was really here in Alaska, somewhere I'd never once thought I'd ever visit. I was about to jump out of a damn plane!

"One... two..." Zana said.

"Oh my God, not yet. Wait, I'm not ready." I needed another minute.

She waited, her hands on my shoulders. I could feel her impatience, but I could also tell she'd wait as long as I needed. Even if I chickened out entirely, she seemed like she'd be okay with that.

I took one more deep breath. "Okay, count again," I squeaked.

"One two *three!*" she yelled out, and launched both of us out of the hatch.

We were in freefall! A scream exploded from my lips as we shot at full speed toward the ground. The snow-covered mountains that had been so distant a minute ago rocketed toward us way too fast. We were going to die! We were going to die! We were going to –

Zana's arm moved behind me, and a parachute popped out of the pack she was wearing. The nylon filled with air, slowing us little by little until we were falling at a comfortable, leisurely pace.

I sucked in ragged breaths as my heart rate started to return to normal. Now that the worst part was over, I could almost relax. We were still suspended in the air, a thin piece of fabric the only thing keeping us from certain death… but the sun shone down on us brightly, and those mountains really were beautiful.

Zana's arms wrapped around my waist, and I

rubbed my head against her neck. We'd made it through this terrifying experience – together.

"How was that?" she asked, her breath hot on my neck.

"Awful. Horrible. I hated it." Our feet touched ground, and I let out a sigh as I found my balance. "When can we do it again?"

THIRTY-ONE – ZANA

Tia's presence didn't quite ruin my weekend, since skydiving – and Lacey – lifted my spirits. Still, I felt much better once the jump was over. I avoided the rest of the group, not even talking to them on the plane ride back to LA.

Lacey and I sat on our own, and I muttered a quick summary of what Tia had said to me. She gasped, her hand over her mouth. "Why didn't you tell me earlier?"

"I didn't want to taint your first skydiving experience," I said.

I'd been unsure about telling her at all, not wanting to hurt her feelings. All of the news articles and online uproar had to be taking its toll on her, even if she didn't show it. I hated to rub salt into the wound by saying my parents didn't want her in my life, either. In the end, I decided honesty was the best policy – I wouldn't have felt right keeping this from her.

"But… what are you going to do now?" she asked. "Your friends, and… your parents?"

It seemed like my friendship with Kaidee, Gemini, and Brittney might be over. They'd seemed happy to have Tia in their group, chatting and giggling through the whole flight. I guessed they'd chosen her over me, after all.

Maybe I should've been upset, but in fact, I couldn't muster up any kind of emotion about them. I'd already given up on their friendship once, and it hadn't bothered me then.

In a thick voice, I explained how my "friends" and I hadn't been talking lately. Lacey had such genuine connections with her friends and family that she had a hard time understanding my relationships – or maybe it was just my own self-consciousness that made me feel awkward about explaining them to her.

"As for my parents, I'll call them when we get back," I said. "I'll tell them to fuck off. It's bad enough that they've been trying to manipulate me directly. It's not acceptable for them to bring other people into this."

"What if they cut you off?" she asked. "What will you do?"

I smiled bitterly. "That's where they messed up. They've been paying me off and bribing me for so long, my bank account is healthy on its own. If they cut me off today, I could still live comfortably for the rest of my life. I might have to rein in my spending a little, but not much. It'd be worth it for the independence. Basically, their money is meaningless to me."

They'd already cut me off once before, when I came out of the closet. We hadn't spoken for weeks, and I hadn't missed them one bit. I hadn't been *happy* about it, but financially and emotionally, I was fine. They'd never been the kind of parents I wanted or needed, anyway.

Lacey squeezed my hand and laid a soft kiss on my cheek. "Whatever you want to do, I'll support you."

*

In the morning, I lay in bed, scrolling through the news as Lacey slept beside me. I did wish I had more people in my life – real, genuine people that actually cared about me – but for the moment, she was all that I needed. I'd take one real her over ten fake friends, any day.

A familiar face popped up on my phone screen – my own. My heartbeat stuttered. I'd already scrolled past the article – I could just keep scrolling. I didn't need to see what kind of negativity the media was spreading. I already knew it was all bullshit.

But some masochistic urge forced me to scroll back up and click on the picture of my own face. *Zana King's Spending Is Out Of Control,* the headline read. The article said I'd dropped ten grand on a date with my new girlfriend.

I bit back my disgust. I should've known something like this was coming.

The article didn't contain any lies, which was both good and bad. Good because the media wasn't spreading crazy rumors with no basis in truth this time. Bad because I was pretty sure Lacey had no idea how much our weekend had cost. She hadn't asked any questions about how much I was charging to my credit card.

There was also the fact that we hadn't actually agreed on the word "girlfriend."

I watched as Lacey slowly opened her eyes. Should I hit her with this now or later? I might as well get it over with and not have it hanging over me until I told her. I kissed her cheek, caressing her with both hands, and then wordlessly handed her the phone.

She blinked as she read the article. "What is this?" she asked, suddenly alert. "Is this true?"

"Which part?"

She sat up sharply. "The part where you spent more on one date than I make in two months. I don't know which other part would be relevant."

"Well…" I grimaced. "You had fun, didn't you?"

"Not five thousand dollars worth of fun! Jesus, Zana, I've been stressing so hard over where to find the money to pay my family's rent, and you drop ten grand like it's nothing?"

My stomach lurched. "How much is your family's rent?"

She got a fierce expression on her face. "You're not paying it for us. Don't even think about it."

"Why not? I'm sure it's not ten grand. You just said yourself, it'd be nothing for me."

"That doesn't matter. It's the principle of the thing."

I got up – walking on both legs! – and went to my little-used office. A minute of digging through the desk drawers, and I'd found my check book. "How much?" I asked, returning to Lacey.

"I'm not taking your money." She'd crossed her arms as if to prove how stubborn she was planning to be. "I'm not going to sink that low."

"It can be a loan, if you want. I don't really care." I signed my name at the bottom and tore the paper off. "Here, I'll leave it blank. Put in however much you need."

She gaped at me. "What if I put in a billion dollars?"

"Then it'll bounce." I shrugged. "And I don't think you'd do that, because I'm pretty sure your rent is somewhat less than a billion."

Slowly, she reached out and took the check. She looked at it for a long moment, her face tight – and then she shredded it into a hundred tiny pieces. "I'm not going to take your money."

"You're only hurting yourself," I said. "I wouldn't give a shit if you took it. Wouldn't even notice the money was gone."

She sighed and shook her head. I wanted to

sigh, myself. If I couldn't get her to accept money to keep a roof over her head, how was I ever going to get her into nursing school?

Even if my parents cut me off, I'd never miss the couple thousand it took to get her through a semester. I wanted to pay for her textbooks and living expenses, too. She shouldn't have to worry about a thing while she studied… but she'd never go for that, not if it was a hand-out.

"So there was nothing else that bothered you about the article?" I asked, trying to sound playful even though my heart was beating harder.

She looked confused. "Like what?"

I turned the phone on again. "Take another look at this paragraph."

She did, then glanced back at me. "What's wrong with it?"

I swallowed. "It calls you my girlfriend."

"Oh." She paused and looked at the phone again. "Oh!"

"I don't know how you feel about that. I mean…"

"I didn't even notice, honestly," she said. "I guess I've been thinking of you that way for a while."

A smile spread across my face. "Oh, really? And you didn't bother to tell me?"

She looked adorably abashed. "I guess I just

assumed…"

"It's okay. Come here, girlfriend." I grabbed her
– both hands! – and pulled her in. "There are
some dirty things I want to do to you right
now."

She kissed me, the taste of her lips lingering
even after she let me go. "Then I guess it's a
good thing I'm your girlfriend."

THIRTY-TWO – LACEY

My mom ended up taking out an advance on her next pay check. Somehow that stressed me out even more. We still had to come up more money next month, and there was no way I'd ever accept a loan from Zana.

I needed to find a job, and quick.

I almost missed the phone call when it came. I was sprawled out on Zana's couch, my head in her lap as we watched an action movie. My phone was on silent, so the only reason I knew it was ringing was that I saw it light up with an incoming call.

Zana followed my gaze. "Don't answer it. Let the voice mail pick up."

"I better see who it is." I picked up. "Hello?"

"Hi, is this Lacey?" a slightly familiar voice asked. "Wendy Jamison here. I'm calling about the care worker position."

I sat up straight. "Yes!" Was she calling to offer me the job, or to tell me I wasn't getting it?

"I've interviewed several candidates now, and none of them have seemed as capable as you. As honest, either. The job is yours, if you still want it."

My jaw dropped. "Of course! Definitely! When

can I start?"

Zana frowned at me, looking confused. "I got the job," I mouthed at her. She pursed her lips without saying anything.

"How does Monday sound?" Wendy asked. "We have a patient whose current care worker is leaving, so you'll be able to jump right in."

"Sounds fantastic! What can you tell me about them?"

Staying as calm as I could, I took mental notes about the patient. Apparently he was a fifty-three-year-old quadriplegic. I was glad I'd asked for details. I'd never worked with a paralyzed person before, and now I'd have a full week to learn and get prepared.

I hung up the phone, still glowing with excitement. "I can't believe she offered me the job!" I said. "We need to celebrate! Do you have a bottle of champagne somewhere in this house? Let's crack some bubbly open!" Any champagne she owned would probably cost more than I'd get in my first pay check, but in this moment of happiness, I was willing to look past that.

"I'll look for some," she said, standing up slowly. She went downstairs, seeming decidedly unexcited.

I grabbed my phone, still bursting with enthusiasm. I shot a quick text to each of my parents, and one to Lonnie as well. His response came back immediately, filled with exclamation marks and sparkling heart emojis.

I looked up to find Zana in front of me. She had a bottle of champagne and two fluted glasses in her hands, but I was more concerned about the serious expression on her face.

"You don't seem happy for me," I said, trying not to sound accusing.

"Of course I am," she said. "Let's pop this open."

I bit my lip. "Are you sure?" I tried to think of why she might not be excited. "I know it's not a lot of money, and I won't be able to spend as much time with you…" If it were up to her, she probably would've just handed me money. She liked it when I never left her side.

Her parents had cut her off until she "came to her senses" regarding me. Neither of us had been surprised. She seemed to be fine with it, but maybe she felt weird about money now. Then again, she hadn't acted weird at all until now.

"I knew you wouldn't always spend all your time with me," she said. "I just don't know if this is what you really want to do."

"Well, of course I'd rather be in nursing school, but it's fine. I'm saving the money. I'll go back eventually, don't worry."

"Okay. Fair enough." She shifted the bottle to her other hand. "I know you wouldn't take my money if I offered it."

"You're not putting me through school, Zana."

"All right, then." She pulled the stopper off the bottle. What should've been a satisfying *pop* was only a quiet fizzle. "I do think you'd be able to help more people if you were a nurse."

"Are we still on this?" I was getting frustrated now. "I got a job. I'm happy. Let's drink the champagne."

"Okay, we're going to drink it." She poured the champagne, and we clinked our glasses without speaking.

*

By the next day, I was officially pumped for my new job. I'd been researching how to care for paralyzed patients all evening, and I'd even reached out to some old coworkers to see if they had any tips to share. This was going to be a new challenge for me, and I was psyched to see how well I could handle it.

Zana was less excited, which got me down a little. I wished she could be happy for me, even if she didn't completely understand. She did her best to pretend she wanted me to take the job, but she definitely hadn't inherited her father's acting skills. I could see right through her, and what I saw hurt me.

We had a mutual lack of understanding. I didn't

see what she wanted me to do. Was I supposed to turn down the job and sit at home with her all day? That might be fun for a while, but not for long. I wouldn't be satisfied by sitting around, not learning or growing. Not helping anyone, living off other people's money... It just wasn't me.

At least my parents were happy for me. They were looking forward to having three incomes again. They didn't really care what kind of work I did, as long as I could help keep a roof over our heads.

In the afternoon, I came back to Zana's, planning to take her out for a walk along the beach. I only had a few days left to spend full-time with her, so I was hoping to enjoy them while still doing everything I could to prepare for the new position.

She called me to the living room, where she had her laptop on her knees. "I just found something cool!" she said, looking brighter than she had since I'd been offered the job. "Take a look."

I grabbed the laptop and scanned through the web page. Apparently she was looking at a scholarship for nursing students who'd had to drop out of school because of financial hardship. I hadn't known that was a common enough problem to need a specific scholarship for it.

"Kind of cool," I said, giving the laptop back to her. "Guess there are a lot of people like me out there."

"People like you? Lacey, it's like this was made for you! You have to apply."

I frowned. "Why would I? I just got a job, finally. I'm not going to give it up."

"But this is better, don't you see? You won't have to wait, and you won't have to work. You could be in school again in the summer semester!"

"If they chose me," I said. "They'll probably have a thousand applicants. I'm sure they wouldn't look twice at me."

"So you are interested?" she asked, her eyes glowing. "Or you would be, if they chose you?"

"No."

"They give you a stipend for your cost-of-living expenses!"

"But I have a new job, and I'm excited to start."

She heaved a sigh. "You had good grades in nursing school, didn't you? You had a well-rounded resume and a lot of personal struggles to overcome?"

I thought of my family's financial situation and my grandmother's dementia. "Yeah, I guess."

"You're like the perfect candidate. This is an amazing once-in-a-lifetime opportunity, and you're going to just let it pass by?"

I made a face. For whatever reason, Zana was certain the Janine Pattinson Nursing Students' Fund was the answer to all my problems. I had a feeling she wouldn't let it go until I applied for it. "The deadline is Thursday, the day after tomorrow. I'm not going to have time to apply, even if I wanted to. Not unless you want me to spend less time with you."

"What if you let me do it?" she asked brightly. "Give me all your transcripts and stuff, and I'll fill it out for you while you do your job preparation stuff. Then you won't have to waste any time."

I could get her to drop this whole thing with no effort whatsoever? "Fine," I said. "You can apply for me."

THIRTY-THREE – ZANA

Lacey had fallen straight into the trap I'd set for her. She'd been more resistant than I'd expected, considering what a great deal I was offering her. But it was nice that she was letting me "put in the application" for her. She wouldn't have to make any effort whatsoever to get the money I was gifting to her.

The web designer I'd hired had done a great job on the site. He'd put it together in a matter of hours, and it looked so realistic I'd actually gotten two legit applications!

I felt a little bad for tricking Lacey, but this was the only way to get her to take the money. Was it really that different if it came from a beneficiary foundation or from me? Either way, the result was the same – that she could go back to school and never have to pay anyone back.

I'd tell her the truth one day. On our deathbeds, maybe. I was sure we'd be together that long.

It was Saturday, and two days had passed since I'd "submitted her application." I was sure real scholarships didn't get approved this fast, but I figured it was possible. I wanted to head off this job thing before it started. If all went well, she'd call in and quit today, and the employer could easily find a new care worker for the patient by Monday.

I waited until the afternoon, when we were having coffee in a nice restaurant overlooking the ocean. We reached for our phones to settle a playful debate, and then I sent her the email I'd written earlier and put on a fake surprised expression.

"There's a new message from that scholarship foundation," she said. "Kind of weird that they're emailing me on a Saturday."

I shrugged. "Open it."

"Maybe later."

"Why wait? Let me open it if you don't want to." I reached for her phone, and she let me take it. I clicked, then gave a loud gasp. "Lacey, this is amazing. They chose you!"

Her jaw went slack. "They did? No way."

"Yes, way. Look at this!" I passed the phone back to her. "They said they love your intelligence, your history, and your drive to succeed. I guess I did a good job on your application!"

She looked at me uneasily. "You didn't bribe them to pick me or something, did you?"

"No." There was no "them," so I wasn't actually lying. "What do you think? Are you going to go for it?"

She seemed less enthused than I would've expected. "I need to read this over and think about it… maybe see how my parents feel…"

"What is there to think about?" I asked, a little too loudly. "This is the kind of luck people only dream about! You have to take it, there's no question about it."

She bit her lip. "I just need a little time to think."

I sat back in my chair, rapidly deflating. Maybe I'd been wrong, and Lacey really did want the caregiver job. Or maybe she didn't like hand-outs from anyone, not just from me. I wouldn't have called a scholarship a hand-out, but that could've been how it looked to her. I just didn't know what was going on in her mind.

"Think away," I said, forcing a smile onto my face. "Make it quick, though. You'll have to decide between the scholarship and the job."

*

Apparently it wasn't as easy a decision as I'd thought. By late that night, Lacey still hadn't made up her mind. I'd asked her what was so hard about the decision a few times, and she just said she was thinking about it. She'd stepped into another room to call her parents, and hadn't said anything when she came back.

"You should call the job first thing in the morning if you decide to quit," I said as we got in bed. "At least they'll have a full day to find someone else."

"I know that," she snapped, and instantly looked regretful. "Sorry, I shouldn't be like that. It's just that that's a bit obvious."

"So what's holding you back from taking the scholarship?" I asked, curling onto my side next to her. "Don't you want to do what's right for you and your future?"

"I made a commitment to the job, and I don't want to go back on it," she said softly. "Especially when Wendy was nice enough to hire me despite my social media scandal."

Oh… I hadn't thought about that. "You have to look out for yourself first, though," I said. "It may not be nice to break your word, but if you don't, you'll be stuck working at that job for months to earn the same amount of money you could get with one reply email. You'll have to wait at least another few months, until the next semester starts. Your whole life will be on hold." I nudged her in the ribs. "And the worst part is, you'll have less time to spend with me."

"I knew that was what it all came down to," she laughed.

"Seriously, they liked you enough to pick you," I said. "Of all the applications they had, they chose yours. They must think you're pretty special."

"Maybe you're right," she said pensively. "I should call and resign from the job. It'll be better to do it now than later."

"That's what I've been telling you." I grinned.

"Mmm…" She rolled onto her back, yawning. "What about you, anyway? We've been so caught up talking about my future, you haven't told me your own plans. Did you register for classes for next semester?"

"No," I said. "I thought about it, and I'm going to take a break for now. Maybe I'll go back later, but I'll wait until I've picked a new major. I'd rather not go back until there's something I actually want to study."

"That makes sense." She snuggled into my arms, her eyes fluttering shut. "Good night, baby. Thank you for pushing me to do this."

I held her tightly, a faint pulse of guilt vibrating through my core. "You're very welcome."

Thirty-Four – Lacey

Wendy was completely understanding when I called and said I wouldn't be able to take the job. Although she sounded disappointed, she said this happened all the time. "If you had another opportunity come up, you should take it. Don't let us hold you back."

I officially accepted the scholarship offer, and within a matter of hours, a lump sum had been transferred to my bank account. It was more money than I'd ever had in there before, and I stared at my computer screen in disbelief. This was only for the first semester, too – I'd have more coming next semester.

I couldn't believe how lucky I was. I wondered how I'd ever considered *not* accepting this scholarship. Why would I have wanted to toil away for months, earning what could be given to me in a heartbeat? I would've been challenged by the care worker position, sure, but nursing school would present a whole new set of challenges.

I spent the next few weeks getting ready for the summer semester. I gathered the textbooks I'd used before and carefully reviewed the notes I'd taken. After registering for my next set of classes online, I went to the on-campus bookstore to pick up the new books I'd need.

With the money I'd been given, I even went on a bit of a shopping spree at the school supply store. New binders, notebooks, pens, paper clips, and stacks upon stacks of pristine lined paper. I fondled the pages as I stood in line, joyful at the possibilities they'd contain.

I wrote my parents a check for my part of the next few months' rent, since the scholarship so generously covered living expenses. I was spending more time at Zana's place than theirs these days, to the point that they were actually talking about downsizing.

Although I still felt like it was too soon for me to move in with Zana, I hoped it'd happen eventually. My parents could find a nice one-bedroom apartment with a much lower rent than our current house. I'd still send them money from my future nursing job to help them out, but it'd be for special luxuries, not to keep the lights on.

I didn't intend to bring up moving in with Zana. I didn't want to look like a gold-digger. But whenever she did bring it up, I'd be ready.

"I've never had a relationship like this before," I told Lonnie as we sat at a bar one night. Now that I wasn't working, I had enough time to hang out with him. "I mean, I've never had any relationships before, but I never even imagined one could be like this."

"What's so great about it?" he asked. "Other than her being super-famous and all."

"Her being famous is the only bad part, actually," I said, twirling my straw in my drink. "It sucks to constantly be careful of what we do and what it might look like if a photo is taken at the wrong time. Other than that, we're perfect together. She's becoming more empathetic, and I'm chilling out a bit. We just fit with each other, like two puzzle pieces that've finally slotted together."

A dreamy smile came over his face. "That was what it was like for me and Mark, and now it's been five years."

I hoped it could be like that for me and Zana, too. At the moment, it seemed possible, or even likely.

"There's no issues with her ex?" Lonnie asked. "They seemed pretty serious, from what I saw in the news."

"I know." I still got insecure when I thought about Tia. Their relationship had been six months, and while that wasn't that long in the grand scheme of things, ours was even shorter. "Things have been pretty calm lately. I heard Tia started dating some other celebrity, so I guess more of the attention is on them."

"That's fantastic. And you're going back to school?" He shook his head. "It's like you're getting everything you've ever wanted."

I knocked on the table. "Hey now, don't jinx me."

*

A full month after being awarded the scholarship, classes were set to begin. I arrived on campus, my senses tingling. I was nervous about going back to school – it'd be a big change from working, and an even bigger change from doing nothing with Zana, as I'd been doing lately.

I was going to have to study like I'd never studied before. The second year of nursing school was no joke, and I was at a disadvantage because I'd been out of school for over a year. Although I'd tried to refresh my memory of the concepts I'd learned before, there was a lot I'd packed into my head, and I wasn't confident that I'd remember all of it.

Before I could go to class, I had to update my student ID card. I went to the registrar's office, where a bored-looking older lady took my name and date of birth. I put my backpack down clumsily – I was going to have to get used to carrying one again. I had the textbooks and notebooks for all the day's classes inside, and it was seriously heavy.

"Great, so that's that," the clerk said. "I just need a picture of you."

I stood in front of the camera, and a giant smile plastered itself over my face.

"Wow, you really look happy!" she said, clicking something on the computer. "Most kids aren't this happy to go back to school."

"Well, I'm twenty-three, not a kid." I laughed. "I had to drop out last year because of my financial situation, which was devastating. I was lucky enough to get a scholarship that's taking care of everything for me, so yes, I'm very happy to be back."

"Sounds like a generous scholarship," the woman said, her eyes still on the screen. "Which one?"

"It's from the Janine Pattinson Nursing Students' Fund."

Her eyes flicked to me, and she frowned. "Never heard of it."

I shrugged. "There are a lot of scholarships out there."

"Helping students get scholarships is another part of my job, so I've heard of most of them." She glanced at the woman at the next desk. "Betty, you ever hear of a Janine Pattinson Nursing Students' Fund?"

"Nope," the other woman said.

A cold fist wrapped around my stomach. "It might be new. I'm not exactly sure." I hadn't done any research on where it came from or who was awarding it. I'd really only looked at the website when Zana had shown it to me, and then all my contact with the organization had gone through her.

"I'll write it down," the clerk said. "Maybe I can recommend it to some other students. Not many scholarships are that generous."

"Right." I forced a smile, and it still came out weak. "That'd be great, just great."

Thirty-Five – Zana

Lacey didn't come over after class, which was odd. Normally she came over every day automatically – we didn't even have to talk about it. She spent half her time at my place these days, and her things were taking up more and more of my closet.

Her last class was over at three – I'd memorized her schedule. She might be in the library studying, of course. She was such an adorable keener. She liked to have dinner at six o'clock, though, so when six came and went, I gave her a call. No answer.

I paced around my ground floor, my stomach slightly queasy. It wasn't like she was missing – she'd only been out of touch for a few hours. She could very well have bought something to eat and gone back to studying. But how much material could her classes have covered on the first day?

I sent her a text. *Hey, just wondering where you are – hope school went amazing!*

Ten minutes passed. Still no answer.

I knew there was most likely an innocent reason for her disappearance, but this was stressing me out. She normally responded quickly when I texted, and I hadn't heard from her at all since the morning.

I grabbed my car keys and headed out the door. If she wasn't here, the next most likely place to find her was her parents' house. Since they liked me, I'd pretend I was casually dropping by.

I arrived at their door half an hour later and checked my phone again. Still no text – I'd been right to come.

I knocked on the door, and Lacey's mom quickly opened it. "Hey, Juliet," I said. "Is Lacey around?"

"Yes." She gave me a curious look, or maybe an uncomfortable one. "She's in her room upstairs. Feel free to go up."

I did, my footsteps slowing as I neared Lacey's room. I'd been so desperate to find her, and now I was nervous, feeling like I'd overstepped. If she hadn't come over or replied to my texts, maybe she was busy – maybe I should've left her alone. Surely she'd understand I'd been worried, though.

I knocked on her door. "I'm in the middle of something, Mom!" she called. Her voice confirmed she was safe and sound, which sent a flood of relief through me.

"It's me, actually. Zana."

A moment passed, and then her footsteps sounded. She opened the door a crack, and her deep brown eyes glared out at me from within. "What are you doing here?"

I stumbled back as if she'd hit me. I'd been right – I was infringing on her by coming here, even if her mom hadn't realized it. "I was worried," I stuttered. "I didn't hear from you. I wanted to check on you."

"Well, I'm here, and I'm fine – not that you care."

"Why wouldn't I care?" Collecting myself, I pushed gently on the door. "Would you let me in?"

"Why? So you can lie to my face some more?" She yanked the door open, making me stumble inside.

I landed hard on my recently-broken leg and grimaced. "What are you talking about?"

"Are you seriously going to act like you don't know, Zana?" Now I noticed her face was streaked with tears. "Or should I call you *Janine Pattinson?*"

My stomach turned over. "Oh."

"So you're not even going to deny it?" She thrust her laptop at me. The website I'd had made was open. "You did this. You tricked me."

My throat was dry. I hadn't planned on her finding out. God… how had she found out? "I knew you wouldn't take my money," I said uncomfortably. "I knew how much you wanted to go back to school. I wanted to see you do it."

"So you didn't talk to me about it or try to

convince me normally." Her face was red, her fists clenched. "You cooked up an elaborate lie instead."

"I wouldn't put it like that…"

"Then how would you put it? Huh?" She pressed her hands to her face, then shook her head. "It doesn't even matter. I'll pay your money back – once I find a job, since you made me turn down the only one I could get. Then I never want to see you again."

My heart stopped. *"What?"* I whispered.

"You lied to me, Zana! Do you understand that?" A tear dripped down her cheek. "I should've trusted what I thought of you at the start. That you were a selfish, entitled brat."

"I only tried to help you."

"Well, you didn't!" Her voice turned into a shriek. "All the bad things that have happened to me lately are because of you. I was only ever in the news because of you, and now I can barely walk out of my house without worrying about paparazzi stalking me. You put me in the middle of a scandal, even when there was none there. Nobody ever hated me before, and now the entire world does. All because *you* wanted me at the Grammys. You, you, you, you, you!"

The blood drained from my face. I'd wanted *her* to have the chance to go to the Grammys. Didn't she see that?

"I'm so tired of feeling insecure next to you," she

said. "I'm tired of going online and reading a million articles about how I'm not good enough for you, how your ex was better for you. Your parents were willing to pay millions to get rid of me, for fuck's sake! I'm sick and tired of trying to fit into a world I'm never going to fit into, and I'm not going to do it anymore. Not for someone who treats me like a child and won't even let me make my own decisions."

"Don't say that." My heart was breaking. "I'll fix everything. I'll make it better – "

"*How?*" she yelled. "You think you can buy your way out of any problem in life. News flash, Zana, you can't. At least not this one. I'm fucking *done*."

The door creaked open, and Juliet's worried face peeked in. "Is everything all right in here, girls?"

I hung my head. It wasn't – not at all – but Lacey had made it clear how she felt, and I wasn't going to stay where I wasn't wanted.

I couldn't pay for her to love me.

"Everything's fine," I said quietly. "I was just about to go."

Thirty-Six – Lacey

Three days had passed since that awful break-up. Three of the most stressful days of my life. I'd returned the money Zana had given me, every penny – which meant I was in debt, since I'd already spent so much of it.

I hadn't been to class, not the first day or since then. I was in talks with the college administration, trying to get the classes refunded and the textbooks returned. If it didn't work out, I'd find some way to pay for them myself. Some way that didn't involve taking a hand-out from Zana.

I never would've thought she'd betray me like that. She knew perfectly well I wouldn't accept the money, and her solution was to lie about where it was coming from? Her logic was bizarre.

"Sweetie, do you want to talk about it?" Mom was at my door again, her face filled with concern. She'd been working nonstop since the break-up, and I'd hardly seen her. "I heard some of the yelling the other day, but I'm not quite sure what happened."

Sighing, I gestured at her to sit on my bed. As concisely as I could, I summarized what'd happened.

"I don't know what I'm going to do about the money," I said. "Where can I possibly find it, now that she convinced me to turn down that job?"

My phone vibrated, and I saw I finally had a new email from my bank. Had Zana accepted my transfer – or had she rejected it? A spark of hope leapt through me. If she rejected the transfer, I'd be stuck with the money, and I could still take the classes without guilt. But no, I'd still be taking her money. I couldn't do that.

Anyway, as I opened the email, I saw she'd accepted the money. A knot grew in my stomach. She didn't need the money – it meant nothing to her – so her accepting the transfer meant she was accepting that I needed to stand on my own two feet. And that I'd broken up with her.

I hadn't meant to go that far. I'd only wanted to yell at her, make her understand how I felt. Then she'd come over here acting all worried about me, and I just snapped. I couldn't deal with her treating me like a child.

I'd done the right thing, though, hadn't I? Things were never going to work out between us. The last few months had been a fluke. Things couldn't have continued like that.

"We'll work things out," Mom said slowly. "You know, it might be time for us to downsize. We've been thinking about that for a while."

"We'd all move into a two-bedroom

apartment?" I asked. It might be a tight fit. Still, it'd work, and it'd definitely be cheaper than this. Lots of families lived in apartments. It'd be fine.

Mom's mouth twisted. "Maybe a one-bedroom, if you don't know when you'll be able to find another job."

"Where will I sleep?" I asked in a small voice.

"We can get you a pull-out couch."

I gaped at her, then bit my lip. She was right. We needed three incomes to survive as a family, and if I wasn't going to bring money in for a while, things would be seriously tight. It'd be better for us to live in a smaller space, rather than having to scrounge for rent every month.

"Okay," I said.

"Of course, that's assuming you won't move in with Zana eventually."

I shook my head, vehemently at first, and then slower. "I broke up with her. It's over."

"I know, but that doesn't mean it has to stay that way. She didn't seem too happy about it. I'm sure she'd take you back."

"I can't ask for her back." My pulse was racing just thinking about it. "I said some horrible things."

"Things you didn't mean?"

"I – I don't know." While I was angry about what she'd done, I hadn't meant to drag all the other stuff into it. The other things weren't even her fault. "You're not just trying to get a rich daughter-in-law, are you?"

She chuckled. "No. I couldn't care less how much money Zana has, as long as she makes you happy. And she does."

She was right about that much.

Mom ran her fingers through her hair. "I know you care about that girl, Lacey. I suspect you even love her. I know she's your first real girlfriend, and that makes things a little more intense. Maybe you don't know this, but it takes time for people to feel each other out and figure out how they should act with each other. What works for one person might not work for another."

"Huh?"

She leaned forward. "Zana had good intentions, sweetie. She was trying to do something nice for you." I started to object, and she cut me off. "I know, I know, it wasn't what you wanted. But you're forgetting it might've been the perfect thing to do for someone else."

Would it have? I tried to imagine someone who'd want to be tricked like that. Well… maybe it was possible. There were people out there who would've taken the money as a gift from Zana, no questions asked.

But my mom wasn't one of them. Neither was my dad. "You don't think I should've taken her money, do you?" I asked. It went against everything they'd ever taught me.

"No," she said. "Is it a deal-breaker, though? I don't know. If you really don't think Zana should be part of your life, then let her go. But couples do fight. Sometimes they even break up, and that can bring them closer together."

"No, it can't," I automatically said.

"It sure can. Did I ever tell you your father and I split up a few months into our relationship?"

I stared at her. "You did?"

"We had a pretty big fight, and I thought it would kill our relationship. But he fought for me, and I decided I'd try giving him a second chance." Her face softened. "That second chance turned into twenty-eight years. If I hadn't given it to him, you wouldn't be here."

I swallowed. "Maybe I should talk to Zana."

She smiled. "You think?"

THIRTY-SEVEN – ZANA

I sat at a bar, staring glumly into my empty glass. After spending the past few days alone in my house, I'd been desperate for human contact. The only problem was that I couldn't stand anyone I knew.

I'd thought of calling up my old friends, but I assumed they were busy hanging out with my ex. I'd even considered running to my mom, but I knew how little sympathy she'd have for my current situation.

Who else was in my life? Only Lacey. I was desperate to talk to her… and she never wanted to see me again.

"Can I get you another?" the bartender asked. A middle-aged woman with a plump face and grey hair, she looked like someone who definitely wouldn't have heard of me.

"Sure," I said. "Another gin and tonic."

"Coming up." She moved a step away and started to mix the drink. "What's on your mind?"

"Oh… nothing."

She gave me a kind smile. "You've been sitting here for two hours, not saying a word to anybody. You're not even looking at your phone, just staring into space. I'm a mom. I can tell when someone needs to talk."

She was too nice. "I wish you could be my mom," I said before I could hold back. The alcohol had loosened my tongue more than I'd realized.

Luckily, she only laughed. "You can think of me that way, if you'd like. My name's Daphne." She reached across the bar.

"Zana." I shook her hand. "I'm just going through a rough break-up. Things were going so well with this girl for a few months, and then I screwed up." I paused to see if she was taken aback by the word "girl." She didn't even blink an eye.

"Did you cheat on her?" she asked.

"No!" I leaned my elbows on the bar. "I would never."

Daphne nodded slowly. "Then maybe it can be fixed."

"I don't know," I said. "She said she never wants to see me again. How am I supposed to do anything now?"

"That is a tough one." She frowned. "You might just have to wait for her to come to you."

That wasn't what I wanted to hear. "What if she doesn't?"

"Then you move on."

My eyes popped. "Move *on?* Like, with someone

else? There's no one else I want. No one in the world could interest me now that I've dated her."

"I think she will come back to you, then," she said. "If your feelings are that strong, hers have to be, too."

I hoped so… but what if they weren't? Lacey was beautiful and strong and caring and independent. What did I have to offer, besides money and fame, which didn't matter to her at all?

"In any case," Daphne said, "I didn't mean you should move on with someone else. You need to move on with your life. As bad as this may be for business, you need to do something besides lurking around in a bar."

I looked down at the drink she'd handed me a minute ago. It was already half-empty. "I do other things."

"Like what?" She had a slightly snarky tone at first, then softened it as she repeated the question. "What do you do?"

"Well… not much," I admitted. "My parents are kind of famous, so I have plenty of money. I was technically in school until recently, but I wasn't going to classes. I decided to stop until I know what I want to do."

"Seems like this is the perfect time for you to figure that out." She rubbed a dishtowel over the counter. "You didn't like what you were taking before?"

"Liberal arts," I said. "I hadn't picked a specialization yet. I thought something would jump out at me as I took more courses – something I could be passionate about. It didn't."

"Maybe you're passionate about something that isn't a liberal art."

"My mom's a singer and my dad's an actor, so a lot of people thought I'd follow in their footsteps, but I wasn't interested in either of those."

"Those and liberal arts aren't the only options out there," she said. "What do you do for fun?"

Spend time with Lacey. "I like to keep active," I said instead. "Skiing, snowboarding, skydiving…"

"Maybe you'd like to be a personal trainer, or something along those lines."

"I don't think so," I snorted. I could just imagine how scandalous it'd be if Colette and Maurice King's daughter turned out to be a personal trainer. "I'm actually a licensed skydiving instructor. Never taught anyone, though."

"Ah, so there's something you like." She eyed me. "Why do you enjoy skydiving so much?"

"I love the adrenaline rush," I said – then paused. There was more to it than that. "I even liked the in-class training. It used some of the physics I learned in high school, but in an interesting way. I wouldn't have minded learning more, if it was all going to be like that."

"So you're interested in physics," she said.

"I guess you could put it that way."

"What kind of job do you think you could get with that?" she asked.

"It doesn't matter. I…"

I trailed off before I could tell her about my famous parents and the piles of money in my bank account. Maybe my career *should* matter, even if I didn't technically need the salary. Was I going to live off my parents forever? Even if I could, did I really want to?

"I hadn't thought about it," I finally said.

We talked for a while longer, discussing my potential career options. I had to admit, I'd never thought about going into science before. It was completely unlike what my parents did, completely unlike what anyone would've expected of me. But that didn't mean anything.

I hadn't tried very hard at any of my subjects in high school. I'd never given science a fair shot, especially physics – the most dry and boring of them all. But in my short skydiving instructor course, I'd been fascinated by the concepts of velocity, terminal speed, and freefall. When those concepts were out in the real world, in a context I found interesting, they weren't boring at all. How had I never realized that before?

Daphne got out her phone to research careers in physics for me, practically ignoring her other customers as she got more and more excited about our discussion. At some point I stopped drinking, and as my mind got clearer, I knew this was something I really wanted to do.

Physics. Who would've thought?

Eventually two o'clock came, and Daphne had to shut down the bar. "Thank you so much," I said, reluctantly standing up. "This has been amazing. This conversation might've changed my whole life."

"You're very welcome," she said. "I'm glad I could help. Good luck with your studies, and with that girl."

"Girl?"

I'd been so focused on the new opportunities I was considering, I'd managed to forget about Lacey. Now her absence hit me again, even harder than before.

I should've been going home to her, excited to tell her all of my new plans. Instead, I'd never be able to tell her I'd found a new path in life.

It was ironic. She'd wanted me to value school, to want to work. I hadn't thought I'd ever change, and in a single conversation, I had.

But she didn't want to hear about it.

Thirty-Eight – Lacey

When I woke up in the morning, the first thought on my mind was Zana. My conversation with my mom came back to me, and with the clarity brought by sleep, I saw she was right. Zana brought so much to my life, and she meant the world to me already.

She cared about me, too. She'd given up so much because of me – her parents' money and her relationship with them. She'd chosen me over her friends and her so-called perfect ex-girlfriend.

I'd been much too hasty about breaking up with her.

What she'd done wasn't cool, and I should've talked it out with her – explained why I was shocked and hurt by her lie. We could've even fought over it without it going as far as it had. I shouldn't have just gone nuclear.

The thought of going through the rest of my life without her gave me a physical pain in my chest. The last few days had been absolutely miserable. I couldn't make it through sixty or seventy years of feeling the same.

I had to win her back. I was fairly sure she still wanted to be with me – but what if she didn't? What if she'd come to her senses? She might've realized she should be with someone more like her, who could pay her own way and who wasn't fazed by all the trappings of celebrity. Hell, she might've even gone back to her ex!

Luckily, I had a convenient way to see what she was up to. I pulled my laptop onto my chest and opened her Twitter. It hadn't been updated in days – weeks, actually. As I looked at the date of her last post, I frowned. She hadn't posted anything since the first few weeks we'd been together. Her last post told the world we were dating, and to stay out of our business. *All I care about now is me and her,* it said.

With guilt tugging at my heart, I typed her name into Google. A new article popped right up. *Zana King Drinks For Hours At Seedy LA Bar.* The text talked about how Zana had been seen going into the bar at seven pm and hadn't left until closing. It speculated that there were issues with our relationship, and questioned whether she could really be happy with someone so far below her status.

I wasn't going to let the cruel words hurt me this time. They rolled off my back like water as the other part sank in. Zana wasn't with anyone else, which was good – but she clearly wasn't feeling too great about our break-up. I'd hurt her, maybe even as much as she'd hurt me.

I showered and got dressed, trying to figure out the best way to approach her. I could probably just go over to her place and tell her I wanted to be with her, but after screwing up like this, I wanted to do something more dramatic. I wanted to *win* her back.

How could I impress the girl who had everything – especially when I had no money? I thought of the grand romantic gestures in movies and TV shows. I wanted to rush up to her in the airport and stop her from getting on that plane – except she wasn't going anywhere, so how was that supposed to work?

I couldn't write her a song when the songs her mom had written about her were full of lies. I couldn't read her a speech when her dad was a famous actor.

The only thing I could think of to do was to show up there. Just me, laying my heart bare to her. No bells and whistles, no fancy tricks.

Just me.

And maybe some cookies.

I spent the morning baking, partly because cookies might butter her up a tiny bit, partly because I was nervous to see her again. I'd been so harsh with her last time, I still wondered if she might yell at me and kick me off her property.

When the oven timer went off, I had no more excuses to delay going. I packed up the cookies – oatmeal chocolate chip, her favorite – and got into my car.

At her place, I rang the doorbell – an odd feeling, since I'd known her buzzer code since day one. I didn't want to overstep when I didn't know if I'd be welcome, so I waited for her to come to the door.

My heart beat harder as I heard her footsteps come closer. The door opened, and my heart nearly stopped entirely. She looked more gorgeous than ever in her sweatpants and T-shirt, her hair up and no make-up on. Her eyes widened when she saw me, and her mouth formed an O.

God, I'd missed that face more than I could say. I wanted to grab her and kiss her, to hold her close and never let her go. But I had to wait until I knew she wanted me to.

"Do you mind if I come in?" I asked softly. "I don't know if there's any paparazzi out here."

"Yeah." Her eyes were bright. "Come on in."

I looked around the surroundings as if I was seeing them for the first time. I'd convinced myself I'd never be here again, so I was dazed to be here again, and to be in her presence. She seemed different somehow, and yet exactly the same. Had the past few days changed her, or was it all in my head?

She hovered at the bottom of the staircase as if she didn't know if she should take me upstairs. It was funny, considering how arrogant she'd been when we met. Now her arrogance was gone, along with even her confidence. She looked younger and more vulnerable, and it hurt to see her like this. I never would've thought I'd say this, but I would've rather had the first, arrogant version of her.

I guessed she didn't know how to act because she didn't know why I was here. For all she knew, I might've come to yell at her some more. I gave her a nervous smile, trying to put her at ease.

"I…" I'd rehearsed all kinds of things I might say, but now that I was here, I was finding it hard to speak. "I…"

Her face softened, then filled with concern. "What, Lacey?" She moved to touch my shoulder, dropping her hand before it made contact.

"I… oh…" It was official, I'd forgotten how to make words. Remembering the foil-wrapped cookies in my hand, I thrust them at her speechlessly.

She took the package and peeked inside. "Cookies? These smell amazing, but…"

I had to pull myself together and say something to her. Maybe even form a full sentence. "These are sorry cookies!" I burst out.

She stared at me.

"Apology cookies," I clarified. "I mean, I'm sorry!"

Her jaw fell slightly open, and she blinked. "Sorry… for… what?"

"For breaking up with you." I let out a huge

breath. My thoughts were finally becoming clearer. "I shouldn't have done that. I was much too hasty, and I didn't even think it through. I was angry at you, but not to the point of breaking up. I don't want to live without you, Zana. I love you."

Her eyes misted over, and she stepped forward, wrapping her arms around me so that her unique Zana scent I'd missed so much filled my nose and made my head spin. A rush of feelings overwhelmed me, happiness and relief and love. She didn't hate me! She wanted me back!

"You were right to break up with me," she said into my shoulder. "I was horrible. I should've been honest with you, and if you were determined to make your own way, I should've respected that."

"You should've, but I was wrong too. I was being silly and stubborn. There was no good reason for me to not take your money, and it definitely wasn't worth breaking up over."

She took a step back so she could look at me again. "I do understand why you didn't want to take it. I really do. Your independence matters to you, and I should never have forced the money on you."

"I just…" I blinked as something clarified in my mind. "I never wanted you to feel like you had to buy my love. At first you were paying me to be with you, and when we started dating, I wanted to completely pull away from that. I wanted you to realize I'd be here if you were poor, even if you were broke. The reason I love you has nothing to do with money."

"Oh, Lacey, I knew that."

"Did you?" I took the cookies she was still holding and set them on a stair, then put my hands on her shoulders. "You were always spending money, taking me on lavish dates. You didn't have to impress me."

"But I would've done the same for anyone I was dating." She looked thoroughly confused.

"Exactly." I let that sink in for a minute, and a look of comprehension slowly dawned on her face.

"You mean... I use money to keep everyone in my life around me. Money and fame."

I nodded. "And those things don't matter to me." I squeezed her shoulder. "They couldn't matter any less."

"I get it now."

She leaned in and pressed her lips to mine, the first time we'd kissed since I'd come here. It felt like kissing her for the first time again, except this time was way better. Our actual first kiss had been fraught with anxiety and insecurity – I hadn't known if she really liked me or what her intentions with me were. Now I knew we were both in love, and we'd be together forever. And the way we clung to each other proved that.

"Things are going to be different from now on," she murmured, wrapping her arms around my waist. "*I'm* going to be different. I'm going back to school for physics, and I'm going to get a job after."

"Did you say *physics?*"

"I'll explain later." One more soft kiss on my cheek, and she pulled away. "I'm going to eat one of these cookies… and then I'd like to take you upstairs."

THIRTY-NINE – ZANA

The cookie was delicious, and Lacey was even better. We stripped off each other's clothes slowly, not because we wanted to take our time, but because we kept pausing every few seconds to make out again, and we couldn't seem to stop long enough to get more clothes off.

I'd missed her lips. Her skin. Her scent. I'd told myself I'd be okay without her, that I'd get over her eventually. Now I knew I'd been wrong. I never could've gone on without her, at least not with my heart whole. She'd kept a piece with her when she broke up with me that day, and only being with her could bring it back.

Both of us were on my bed, me on top of her. I kissed my way down her neck, relishing the way my lips made her squirm. Heat was building between my thighs, and I was sure she felt the same. Her hips bucked toward me as if begging me to touch her, and I wasn't going to make her wait for long. I had so much to make up to her.

I tugged off her jeans and made my way back to her lips, kissing her with all the passion that I felt. Her silky panties were already wet as I slid my hand between her legs, and she moaned into my mouth as I toyed with her.

My heart was so full, fuller than it'd ever been before. Even if we hadn't been together all that long, I knew this was the real thing. Being with my other girlfriends had never felt anything like this. With Lacey, I felt like a key, and she was the lock. We fit together perfectly. We weren't meant to be apart.

I had to break free of kissing her so I could get her panties off. I dropped between her legs, but she stopped me with a wordless sound. She seemed shy to tell me exactly what she wanted, but with timid glances and hand gestures, she guided me to straddle her face.

Ah… she wanted both of us to pleasure each other. We hadn't done this before, and I wondered excitedly if she'd been thinking about it, if she'd been turned on at the thought. I wondered if she'd been disappointed, after breaking up with me, to know we'd never be able to try this together.

The soft warmth of her tongue made contact with my center, and I remembered that none of that mattered.

I lowered myself down, finding that my torso fit perfectly against hers, and that my face fell directly between her legs as if we'd been made just for this. I laughed to myself – that was what I'd just been thinking, that we were two puzzle pieces slotting together. But I couldn't laugh for long when her musk was in my nose, her folds just inches away.

I'd been dying to taste her for days, not knowing if I'd ever get the chance again. Now I could barely savor her sweetness on my tongue because of the way she was working her magic on me.

Our heavy breathing turned to moans, both of us keening louder and louder. My arousal mounted, my core tingling, and I could sense my climax wasn't far off. I wanted her to get there first, though. I wanted her to come for me.

Once her hips began to tremble, I knew I had her at the edge. I gripped her hips and licked her harder, knowing when it was too much for her to take, she'd stop doing anything to me. Except she didn't. She kept doing what she was doing, and I couldn't hold back. My orgasm took over, and she was moaning into me, and the waves of ecstasy went on… and on… and on.

*

We spent the rest of the day in bed together, along with most of the night. We did pause to eat, ordering in take-out from her favorite Chinese place. We tried to go to sleep around eleven, but found ourselves still awake and craving more of each other.

I couldn't get enough of her. I'd said that before, as I'd said I loved her before, but now both sentiments were on a whole other level. Losing her, even only for a few days, had made me appreciate her so much more.

At some point, we stopped for long enough to talk about the future. "You'll move in with me, won't you?" I asked, caressing her hair.

"I'd love to." She smiled up at me. "Where are you going to study? Maybe we can commute together."

"I still have to figure that out."

"And why *physics?*" She sounded incredulous again. "That was the last thing I ever expected you to say."

I started to explain, but halfway through the story of the wise bartender, I got the urge to touch her again, and as soon as I was doing that, I couldn't help but taste her, too.

Eventually, my body was worn out. I didn't know about her, but I simply couldn't take any more. After she brought me to one last shuddering orgasm, I curled into a ball, and her arms wrapped around me from behind. As darkness crept over me, all I knew was the safety and warmth of her cradling me.

She was back here with me. Everything was exactly how it should be.

FORTY – LACEY

The media had a field day with us over the next few months.

Zana King Spotted On-Campus At UCLA – Wild Child Gone Good?

Zana King Snubs Ex-Girlfriend At Nightclub

Moving Vans Outside Zana King's Mansion As Lacey Howard Moves In

I was a household name by this point, which felt extremely odd. People had recognized me on campus, even when Zana wasn't around. As for her, she wore a baseball cap and sunglasses to school, and she'd stopped dying her hair blonde, which made her a bit less recognizable. Her classmates knew who she was by now, but she said they were getting used to her presence.

The media attention did calm down a bit as we settled into our new lives of studying and living together. We were boring now, after all. What was there to say if a photographer spotted us at the library or walking to the parking lot after class? There was nothing juicy there, no drama.

The world had given up on Zana and Tia getting back together. It'd taken some time, but it seemed like people had accepted that she and I were better together – or at least, that she liked me better. Like she'd said from the beginning, things had eventually blown over.

Every now and then, there were even articles about how adorable we were together. There'd be a picture of us holding hands in line at the campus coffee shop, or her rubbing my shoulders as I stared into a textbook. But neither of us minded those, even if they did make us feel a little funny.

We were too busy being happy together. Now that we lived together, we still squabbled occasionally. Nothing like before, though. We both appreciated each other's presence in our lives, and her mansion gave us plenty of space when we needed some time apart.

Once Zana's parents no longer saw me as bad publicity, they reached out to see if the two of us would have dinner with them. According to Zana, their plan was to tip off the paparazzi and have pictures taken. She said no, but I suggested that we join them for Christmas and Easter – no cameras in sight. Things were somewhat tense, considering their history with me. But it was a first step toward them forging a relationship with Zana outside the spotlight.

She and I were in the news again when I graduated from nursing school. The article talked about how much I glowed as I walked across the stage to accept my diploma. There was also a lot of happiness for us when we got married in a low-key, private ceremony in the Cayman Islands. Other than that, we weren't exciting enough to bring much attention anymore. We weren't up to anything scandalous.

We were close to flying under the radar by the time Zana finished her four-year physics degree. She'd ended up focusing on astrophysics, which made us both laugh considering she'd tried so hard to get away from "stars." She'd been a good student – not an excellent one by any means, but she enjoyed the subject, and with my prodding, she'd studied enough to have a solid 3.7 GPA by the time she was done.

As her graduation date neared, we started to think about the future in a way we hadn't before. She wasn't sure what kind of career she wanted, just that she definitely wanted one. After living a life of luxury when she was younger, she'd gotten used to exercising her brain every day, and she said she couldn't go back to how she was before.

"I can't stand living off my parents' money anymore," she said one day as we floated in her indoor pool. "This house, this lifestyle… I guess it's your influence. I want to be independent, like you."

"How would you do that?" I asked, frowning.

"I was thinking…" Her cheeks went pink, and she sank deeper into the water. "I'd like to give away the money they've given me. Everything that's in my bank account. A charity could use it to make a real difference in the world."

I couldn't believe what I was hearing. "And then

what?" I asked.

"Then I'd get a job and live off my salary, just like everybody else."

I didn't honestly think she'd follow through on the idea – but once she graduated, she made a huge donation to an organization supporting LGBT rights in developing countries. She said that preventing people like us from being persecuted was more important than having a lavish lifestyle.

We were both over the glitz and glam of LA in general. At dinner, night after night, we debated what kind of job she should get and where we should move to. The major question was where we might find the quieter life we both craved.

"We should move to some small town in the middle of nowhere," I told her. "Maybe in the Midwest. No one will know us there. No photographers, no paparazzi. We can be anonymous."

"The Midwest, though?" She wrinkled her nose in the adorable way I'd completely fallen in love with. "It doesn't sound too fun."

"What would be fun, then?" I rolled my eyes. "You're so picky. You know, we should just move to Alaska."

She put down her fork. "Alaska?"

"I was joking."

"No, but really." Her eyes went dreamy. "We

had such an amazing time there. That was one of our first dates, don't you remember? Your first time skydiving."

"Sure, but that doesn't mean I want to move there. We'd freeze."

"We'd keep each other warm." She leaned toward me, putting her hand on mine. "It'd be amazing. We could ski and snowboard to our hearts' content, skydive every weekend…"

"Do you think we'll be able to afford that?"

"Of course," she said. "There'll be plenty of nursing jobs in Alaska, and I'll be working, too. We'll get a smaller place up there – we don't need all of this."

She sounded serious about this… and her enthusiasm was starting to rub off on me. It did sound romantic, moving up there to lead a simple kind of life. Nobody would know us in Alaska, and if they did, they wouldn't care.

It felt like a world away from here, and a change could be exactly what we needed.

"We could visit," I said. "Check out what it might be like to live there."

"Yes!" she shouted.

"I'm not committing to anything," I said. "We're *just* going to check it out."

"Sure, we are." She winked.

Epilogue – Zana

"Honey! I'm home!" Lacey called.

I stood up from my computer desk, and Mali ran toward Lacey's voice. He hurried down the staircase in a blur of black-and-white fur. As soon as he reached her, he hopped up and down with excitement.

It'd been four months since we moved to Alaska, and I was happier than I'd ever been. Lacey and I had found a gorgeous house in downtown Anchorage, and we'd adopted a puppy as soon as we moved in – an Alaskan Malamute, naturally.

"Hey, sweetie." I gave Lacey a long kiss. "How was work?"

She'd easily found a job nursing at the local hospital. Her coworkers were great, and the work kept her on her toes. Sometimes she hardly had to do anything all day, and sometimes one patient after another would come in with severe frostbite or wounds from a dog-sledding accident. The only bad thing was that it kept her away from me for hours at a time.

"Great," she said. "How about you?"

I was offering my services as a freelance astrophysics consultant. The work was all online, so I got to sit around in my pajamas, just like the old days. My services were getting a good reputation, so I already had several clients. I still had some quiet days, but if things kept going like this, I'd be working harder than I'd ever worked before. And I didn't mind that idea.

"Not bad," I said. "Come sit down. I want to talk to you about something."

"Is it about Penny's surprise party? Because Dora already texted me to let her know."

Penny and Dora were friends we'd made in town – real friends, the kind who stuck by you through all of your ups and downs. They were around our age, and we all got along, so we double-dated every week or two. They'd both grown up in Alaska, so they already knew a lot of people here, and they'd welcomed us into their community.

"No, it's not about the party," I said.

"Was there something about us in the news?" she asked. "You look serious."

We hadn't been in the news for quite a while now. It seemed that the media wasn't desperate enough to know what we were doing to send reporters all the way to Alaska. And we liked it that way. I'd even deleted my Twitter and Instagram accounts. Lacey and I were too busy being happy for real to put on a show for social media.

"It's not about the news," I said. "I just had some thoughts for the future."

I led her into the living room, Mali darting after us. I'd ordered a package by air-delivery a few days ago, and it'd finally come today. Living in the forty-ninth state had taught me patience. We were a long way from the lower forty-eight, and delivery took a long time. No matter how much money I threw at people, there was no way to get things faster – short of commissioning a helicopter, which I'd actually considered for this particular delivery.

"What is this?" Lacey asked, looking at the binder's cover – *Home Insemination Made Easy: A Kit and Catalogue.*

I thought it was pretty self-explanatory, but I explained anyway. "It's for us to expand our family, Lacey. I'd like for us to have a child."

Her face froze. Had I really taken her by surprise? We'd talked about this before, even if it was a big step to actually order the kit. I was twenty-seven and she was twenty-nine now, and we'd been together for six years. It wasn't crazy to start seriously thinking about growing our family.

"I want that, too," she said slowly. "But how is it going to work?"

"We look through this binder, pick out a man, and order his sperm." I opened the box and pulled out a syringe. "We load it up in here, and – "

"Ew! Too much detail," she laughed. "I mean more like, which of us is getting pregnant?"

She wasn't shooting down the idea, and that lifted my spirits as I answered. "Either," I said. "I don't mind. I'm pretty scared, but I'd be willing to try."

"Me too," she said. "I don't know what to expect, but women have been doing it since the dawn of time. I'd give it a try."

"Maybe you should do it," I said. "At least the first time. Then I could wait on you hand and foot."

She snorted. "Like I used to do for you when we met?"

"Exactly," I said. "I still don't feel like I've made that up to you."

She got an evil smile on her face. "So if I was pregnant, I could order you around and be a total and complete asshole to you?"

"Yup."

"Zana, bring me chips!" she said in a high-pitched voice. "Zana, brush my hair!"

I cringed. "Go for it." I still got embarrassed when I thought about what a jerk I'd been to her when we first met. I'd been young and dumb, and in a lot of pain, but that didn't excuse my bad behavior. I'd never treat anyone like that again.

"Yeah, right." She patted my shoulder. "I give it a week before you give up and hire me a home care worker."

"As if I'd do that!" I sputtered, and put my hand on her knee. As if on cue, Mali came over and laid his head on her other leg. "We're doing this, though?" I asked softly. "We're going to have a baby?"

Lacey nodded, her eyes shining. "I can't think of anything I'd rather do."

I hope you enjoyed reading Scandalous!

Sign up to my newsletter at **http://eepurl.com/dMjIYo** to hear about my new releases.

If you loved the book, please tell your friends! You can also leave a review on Amazon or Goodreads.

Turn the page for a look at my other books.

Thank you for supporting an independent author!

Two Moms

Being a single mom is far from easy, as both Samantha and Joy know. When Samantha's daughter babysits Joy's son, the women are instantly drawn to each other. Each has her own past, but together they have a chance to create something new. Could these two moms end up starting their own family?

Another Mother

Average suburban mom Sarah is suddenly rocketed into the glitzy world of film when her daughter Emma becomes an actress. The strangest part is seeing gorgeous, glamorous Katie Days pretend to be Emma's mother. Sarah is a normal person and Katie is a celebrity, yet they find common ground in the little girl. Could Emma's fake mom become her other mother?

The Marriage Contract

Twelve years ago, Poppy and Leah vowed to get married if they were both single at thirty. After losing touch, the unlikely pair reconnects just in time to meet the deadline. A lot has happened in twelve years... like both of them coming out of the closet. Now the popular girl marrying the science geek is an actual possibility. The contract was only a joke, though - wasn't it?

Shatter Me

Volunteering at a women's shelter, Sydney is shocked to see her former student walk in. She knows Lora is kind-hearted, mature, and capable - but that didn't save Lora from abuse. Sydney becomes a mentor to Lora, and then a friend. Lora finds herself falling for the professor's brilliant mind and caring nature. Can she learn to love again after being shattered once?

Printed in Great Britain
by Amazon